Read what othe

Feeling l

"A woman's hormones don't decline because she ages; a woman ages partly *because* her hormones decline! By reading this book you will begin to understand what happens to your body as you enter your forties and beyond. This is not a technical book. It is written to empower you with the knowledge that something can be done. It is written to motivate you to take the steps to gain back control of your body and mind. Ivy's simple wisdom and guidance inspires every woman to be the best she is capable of being at any age. I highly recommend *Feeling Funkabulous*."

Sangeeta Pati, MD, FACOG

Medical Director, Sajune Medical Center, Orlando, FL

"Ivy has done an excellent job of showing us that life doesn't stop at middle age. My wife, Ruth, is a perfect example. After raising 19 children she still had the time to write books and acquire her Ph.D. in her sixties. Don't hold back. Go for it!"

Pat Williams

Senior Vice President, Orlando Magic

"*Feeling Funkabulous* is refreshing and positive. The story line has valuable lessons for every woman. Ivy has wonderful advice. Listen to her."

Birgit Zacher Hanson, M.S.

Co-Author of *Who Will Do What By When?*

"Ivy's writing is always inspiring, and *Feeling Funkabulous* is no different. The book is uplifting, positive and motivating. It will help every woman to feel better about herself."

Dr. Sheri Lerner

Author of *Bouncing Back from Pregnancy*

"Feeling Funkabulous is an easy read that will shift your consciousness to one of happiness, life satisfaction and abundance. I highly recommend this terrific book."

Ken Donaldson, M.A., L.M.H.C.

Author of *Marry Yourself First!*

"Ivy has crafted a beautiful story interwoven with Lumi Powers' journey from feeling funky to feeling fabulous. Her story will resonate with women of all ages, but especially with women who are forty-something. This is a book you'll remember for a very long time. Don't buy just one copy; buy one to keep and one to give to a friend."

Alice Anderson, Ph.D.

Author of 50 Books in 12 Years

"As I read *Feeling Funkabulous*, I could more than relate... despite being a 'specialist' in the field of menopause, and particularly menopause-related skin and beauty changes. A woman can know everything there is to know about the subject, but going through the actual journey can be a daunting experience. Ivy helps you on this journey and shows you ways to make it even better."

Carrie Pierce

Co-Author of, *Making Peace with Menopause - Embarking on the Journey of your Lifetime and Living to Tell the Tale*

"Age is a mindset. You are only as old as you think you are. Life is fulfilling at any age. Ivy shows you how to get through the challenges and move forward with confidence."

Joe Simonetta

Author of *Seven Words That Can Change the World*

"It is sometimes a struggle getting through the funky years, but Ivy shows you how to do it with grace, dignity and positive thinking."

Dr. Jim Vigue

Award-Winning Author of *Where Did My Wife Go?*

"Ivy shows you that life doesn't have to end with peri-menopause or menopause. The truth is life can still be juicy after the age of forty!"

Debra Smith

The Sensuality Sage

FEELING FUNKABULOUS

From Funky to Fabulous After Forty

Ivy Gilbert

Power Publications, Inc.
Longwood, FL 32750

In view of the complex, individual nature of health, physical and mental problems, this book, and the ideas and suggestions, are not intended to replace the advice of trained medical professionals. All matters regarding health require medical supervision. Seek a physician's advice before beginning any program or programs described in this book. The publisher and author disclaim liability arising directly or indirectly for any psychological or medical outcomes that may occur as a result of following any of the suggestions in this book.

Published by Power Publications, Inc.
ISBN 978-0-6154028-3-3

Photography by Kailyn Gilbert-Vigue

Printed in the United States

Dedication

To all the women in my life:
My daughter, Kailyn
My mother, Jane
My sisters, Sherry, Holly and Stacy
And all of my Fabulous Female Friends.

In Memory of

Marty Simmons and Steve Viola

Two special people who lived their lives to epitomize what true friendship is all about

Acknowledgements

First to Dr. Sangeeta Pati for helping me through my own medical issues and opening my eyes to bio-identical hormones and nutritional supplementation. You are a beacon of light for women everywhere, and the work you are doing is of utmost importance. You are a blessing to so many. May you receive an abundance of blessings back.

To my beautiful daughter, Kailyn, you have more talent than a professional editor, and the corrections and comments you contributed to this book were invaluable. I'm so grateful for you, and I love you with all my heart.

To my son and friend, Kris, thank you for supporting me in every aspect of my life and believing in me, this book and every endeavor. I love you and appreciate that you are always there for me.

Alice Anderson, since my first book, you've been my writing sounding board. With this book you were the catalyst to make me take it off the shelf and complete it. Thank you for the push and jump start.

To the women who first read my book and who gave me advice and input before finalizing it: Crystal Lang, Kristen Becker and Pamela Gasser. Thank you all for taking the time and sharing your thoughts with me. Your input was priceless.

Mom and Dad, you are my ultimate fans of all that I do. Thank you for your love, support and acceptance in every endeavor.

To my inner circle of friends, thank you for your support and friendship.

And last, but far from least, Barry Myers. Together we had a dream, and together we pursued it. Whenever I stopped believing, you believed for me. Thank you for seeing, believing and achieving with me and for loving me throughout the process.

Table of Contents

Introduction

On the first day of May I remember flipping my wall calendar and staring at the page of square boxes numbering from one to thirty-one. *Thirty days*, I thought. There were only thirty days left before I hit the big 4-0! I told myself that all those depressing stories about turning forty didn't apply to me. Forty was going to be great!

And turning forty *did* feel great. But as the months went on, and then the years, I finally had to admit to myself that something had changed within me. Maybe there was something *real* to this *forty-funk* I had heard so much about.

After much reading and research I found that for many women the *forty-funk* begins in their late thirties. For others it's in their forties; and some are fortunate enough not to experience it until their fifties. The extremely lucky are those who never experience it, yet it seems they are fewer in number. Unfortunately, the truth of the matter is that most women *do* find that changes take place within their bodies and within their minds at some point during these years. Very few escape the *forty-funk.*

During this time a woman begins to ask herself questions such as:

- What is my purpose in life?
- Who am I really?
- What do I want to do?
- Am I happy?

Plus there are adjustments needed such as:

- Adjusting to the children' growing up and leaving home.
- Adjusting to a new *over-40* lifestyle.
- Adjusting to the physical changes to one's body.
- Adjusting to changes within one's mind, thoughts and attitudes.

Today turning forty is often the age that a woman uses to define the difference between being a young woman or a more mature one. It becomes a time of reflection—making note that according to statistics this is the half-way point in one's life. It's the bridge that a woman stands on where she reflects on the past forty years of her life and prepares for the next forty. If we were to have lived in the late 1800s, then this change may have been perceived to have come when a woman was fifteen years old, as the life expectancy was only thirty years. In 1900 it would have come at the age of 23, as the life expectancy was 47 years of age. Today in the United States, however, if you are female, life expectancy is over eighty years; so it only makes sense that forty is the age that defines that bridge into the second phase of a woman's life.

However, you must not confuse entering this phase with reaching menopause. This is *not* just about becoming menopausal. It's about *real* changes that a woman experiences that make her feel *off,* out-of-sorts, not herself—simply *funky*—even *before* she enters menopause. The *forty-funk* defines the period of time in a woman's life when it is difficult to pinpoint specific causes or reasons for *real* changes to her body and mind.

The transformation that a woman goes through around this age can be a bit overwhelming and confusing, and until recently all I ever heard were the sad, depressing and frustrating stories of women who had reached this chasm. But I knew that if there was a negative to this period in a woman's life, there must also be an equal positive to it. So I tried to find it.

I won't sugar-coat the reality of being over forty and the true physical changes that take place in a woman's body and mind during this time. Yet I do believe that if you change your focus in a few specific areas, and remember some of life's little lessons, you will be able to change the *forty-funk* into something that is quite *fabulous*. The *forty-funk* should never be an obstacle to your happiness or to living your life as fully as you were meant to live it. But that's ultimately up to you. It's your own personal journey. I know that with a little knowledge, positive attitude, understanding and encouragement, this can be the best time of your life! This book is simply written to give you a little push in that direction and to help you in *Feeling Funkabulous!*

THE FUNK

Chapter One: The Physical Funk

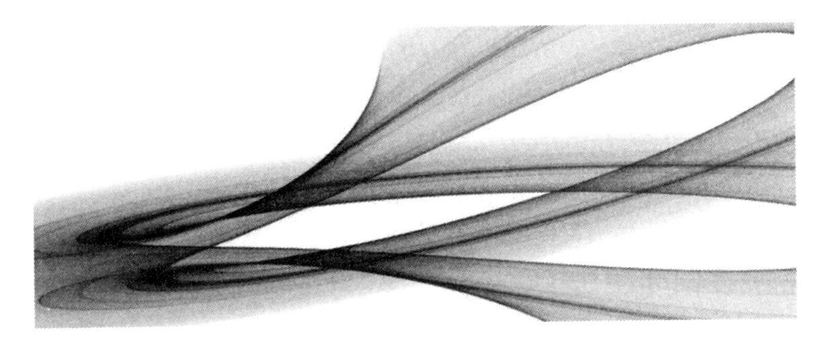

"When a woman reaches 26 in America, she's on the slide. It's downhill all the way from then on. It doesn't give you a tremendous feeling of confidence and well-being."
Lauren Bacall

On the dark cherry night-stand next to her bed, the red luminous numbers on the small digital clock glowed brightly. She tossed and turned most of the night, and even though she had yet to open her eyes, she was wide awake. She lay there silently for twenty minutes or more. She knew it still wasn't even five A.M. or time to get up. It seemed that each night she found it harder and harder to catch her forty winks, which was both frustrating and tiring. She rolled to her right and opened her eyes to a squint just to check the time. The big red numbers on her clock simply confirmed what she already knew—4:45 A.M.

Lumi rolled back onto her pillow and lay quietly for a few more moments to give her some time to think about her day and what lay ahead. A few salty tears trickled down the sides of her cheeks. *Snap out of it,* she scolded herself as she threw her feet over the side of the bed. The tile floor felt cold as she walked quickly to the bathroom. She closed the door behind her, flicked on the light and turned to face her reflection in the large mirror. Looking back at her was an attractive woman with shoulder-length brown hair, big brown eyes and soft lines around her mouth and eyes that had been caused by over forty years of big, bright smiles. That was the image projected in the mirror, but this was not the vision that Lumi saw. What she saw was an unattractive, middle-aged woman with cavernous crevices on her face, gray hairs and way too many extra pounds of fat on her body. *When did this happen,* she thought as she quickly turned away? *It's way too early in the morning for this image!*

That was the image projected in the mirror, but this was not the vision she saw.

She looked down to the floor. There in her line of sight was the bathroom scale staring at her like a judgmental jury. She raised one foot tentatively and placed it on the hard, white metal surface. The numbers started flashing like a neon sign as they zoomed upward. She pulled her foot quickly from the surface of the scale not wanting to know where it was going to stop, because it would be well beyond any number she would be proud to see. She didn't need this digital machine telling her something she already knew: She weighed more than she wanted to. Though she was only five feet four inches tall with a petite frame, she was still about fifteen pounds heavier than she had ever been in her life. Even though she knew that a woman's body changes around the age of forty, she had hoped it was a myth. She hated the thought that she was now one of *those* women who had reached this critical juncture in her life.

Even though she knew that a woman's body changes around the age of forty, she had hoped it was a myth.

She scuffled to the kitchen, got her favorite mug out of the dishwasher, rinsed it, and with a silent blessing for her automatic coffee pot, poured herself a hot cup of coffee. She plunked down at the kitchen table in front of her laptop, where it still sat from the night before. Sipping her coffee slowly while waiting for the computer to boot up, she wondered if she could find information about feeling funky, because there was no other word to describe how she felt, and she wanted to talk to her doctor about it at her nine o'clock appointment.

Clicking away in Internet Explorer on her computer, the first item that came up was a blog about turning forty. She read about weight gain, brain fog, bone decline, gray hair and skin aging, decreased sexual function, mood swings, and changes in energy and sleep. There were stories from women who didn't like what they saw in the mirror, how their skin was no longer tight, how wrinkles were appearing around their eyes and mouths, and how some even had discoloration of their skin or acne once again. Coloring the hair became an automatic six-week ritual to hide the gray. Others regularly forgot why they walked into the kitchen or where they left their keys. *What about sleepless nights?* Lumi thought, as she clicked on another link. Up came numerous articles on changes in a woman's sleep habits and energy levels and how that produces stress. She read how these things contribute to lack of sexual drive and numerous mood swings. *I can relate to that*, she thought. There seemed to be more information about weight gain than anything else. She thought, *The less I eat, and though I have the diet of my neighbor's pet rabbit, I still can't lose weight.* This seemed to be the most frustrating of all symptoms. *Oh yeah, men lose their asses, and women gain them!*

Lumi had simply accepted that these changes were part of the aging process and that she had to endure the transformation that was taking place in her body. She became complacent and discouraged, believing there was nothing she could do. She accepted the physical changes.

She felt she lost control. Her body had won. She had given in to the *forty-funk.*

Glancing at the clock, she couldn't believe how long she had been sitting at the computer. The time had flown and if she were to make her appointment with Dr. Vida, her gynecologist, she would need to hurry up, shower and get ready.

Finally ready to leave, she placed her purse on her shoulder, readjusted her jacket and took a last look in the hall mirror before leaving. She stood there observing the reflection she saw…studying it…assessing every aspect. *God,* she thought, *I need to go on a diet and get my hair colored. I look frumpy and ugly.* Staring more intently she examined the lines on her face. *My wrinkles are the size of the Grand Canyon! I hate who I've become!* And for the second time that day, tears ran down her cheeks, and then she completely broke down. She knew she had find out what was happening to her.

At five minutes to nine Lumi walked into Dr. Vida's office at 1800 7th Avenue. Her eyes were drawn to the water flowing down the wall in a beautiful encased waterfall, and she felt a second of peacefulness and unexplained relief. Her thoughts were interrupted by a bubbly, "Good morning!" from the receptionist. She turned and without looking at the woman from whom the greeting came, she responded with a muffled, "Good morning." She picked up the pen on the counter and signed her name, Lumi Powers, on the pad before her. As she turned to sit down in the waiting area, Dr. Vida came from her office and, noticing Lumi, walked to her and embraced her with an endearing hug.

"It's so good to see you again," Dr. Vida said. "It's been years. Come on in, and let's talk."

Having been put completely at ease, Lumi gladly followed the doctor to her office. They sat down side by side in comfortable, oversized leather chairs as if they were just two friends chatting, not doctor and patient. Dr. Vida was born in India, had beautiful dark eyes, flawless skin and a radiant smile. She was about the same age as Lumi, yet appeared much younger. As they talked casually, Dr. Vida was really beginning her assessment of Lumi's current condition.

"So tell me what's going on," she began.

Lumi began to reiterate all of the information she found on the Internet and how it related to her own issues. She attempted to explain how she felt physically and mentally, and within minutes Dr. Vida knew exactly what needed to be done.

She explained that the underlying root of her *forty-funk* issues was simply all the changes *within* her body (both mentally and physically) that ultimately caused *outward* effects and transformations.

She went on to explain that what was happening to Lumi was perfectly normal—simply an imbalance and decline of hormones and nutrients. Simple tests would confirm the actual levels, but this was something that happened to all women as they age. But the good news, and news that resonated with Lumi, was that these imbalances and deficiencies could easily be corrected, which would help restore her body to a more optimal and youthful state.

"Women age and experience physical symptoms because hormones decline, not the other way around. Let me repeat that statement due to its importance: Our hormones don't decline because we age. We *age* in part because our hormones decline," She also mentioned that another critical factor of restoration of the body to optimal health is by using the powerful effects of the mind.

Our hormones don't decline because we age. We age in part because our hormones decline.

Dr. Vida gave Lumi some reading material that described some of the funky symptoms she was feeling and the related hormonal and nutrient deficiencies that caused them. She summarized by saying, "Hormonal decreases, deficiencies, and imbalances begin around age thirty. By the time a woman is age fifty her hormone levels and function have reduced by approximately 50%. There *are* true physical changes taking place within the body as hormone levels change. By correcting these deficiencies and re-establishing a balance, the body can achieve more optimal performance and get back to what it does best—keeping us healthy and feeling younger and more balanced."

The doctor smiled brightly as she continued, "Forget any comments that you can't defy age, there is nothing you can do about it, or my least personal favorite, it's all in your head. Times have changed. A lot has been learned about aging since your mother's day, and there *are* things that you can do to help rectify, reverse and repel aging. No longer do you have to surrender to the effects of growing older. Everything begins from within, and the first step is to correct imbalances and deficiencies of hormones and nutrients in order to restore your body to an optimal working level. It *can* be done!"

> *Forget any comments that you can't defy age, there is nothing you can do about it, or my least personal favorite, it's all in your head.*

Lumi sat patiently in her chair and examined the wall of medical credentials while Dr. Vida wrote out a script for blood work. She also scheduled another appointment for the same time two days later, and a second one in two weeks. To get her started on the road to feeling better, Dr. Vida outlined a two-week regimen of detoxification, nutrient supplementation and hormonal replacement. Though it all appeared a bit daunting, at least Lumi began to have a small sense of hope.

As she left the office Lumi worried that this would be yet another unsuccessful attempt at feeling better. She had tried numerous diets before with no luck. Exercise never seemed to work out for her. The treadmill she bought was currently a clothes hanger, even though she had promised herself she would use it religiously. *Was this just going to be another time I get excited about something only to be let down again?* She wondered. *Will I have the discipline to do what Dr. Vida is asking of me?* Though Lumi felt a glimmer of hope, her feelings of discouragement and doubt that anything could possibly make her feel better again were quickly rising to the surface. *Oh well,* Lumi thought, *it probably won't work, but I'll give it a try regardless.*

Illumination

As women grow older, hormones and nutrients begin to decline. The result of this decline is a whole host of symptoms that most women simply consider part of the normal aging process. Some of these symptoms, along with the hormone or nutrient deficiency that causes them, are outlined as follows:

Funky Symptom	*Related Key Hormonal and Nutrient Deficiencies*
Aging	*Progesterone, Estrogen, Testosterone, Thyroid, DHEA, Melatonin, Insulin, Growth Hormone*
Bleeding Irregularities, Heavier Bleeding, Bloating, Menstrual Cramps	*Progesterone*
Bone Loss, Joint and Bone Pain, Muscle Weakness	*Progesterone, Estrogen, Testosterone, Growth Hormone, Calcium, Magnesium, Vitamin D*

Cognitive Decline, Brain Fog, Memory Loss	*Estrogen, Testosterone, Thyroid, Pregnenolone, B-12, B-6, Folate, Anti-Oxidants, Iodine, Zinc, Selenium*
Fatigue and Decreased Energy	*Thyroid, Serotonin, B-12, B-6, Iodine, Zinc, Selenium*
Feeling of Being Cold	*Thyroid*
Fibroids, Breast and Ovarian Cysts	*Progesterone*
Hair Loss	*Thyroid*
Higher Cardiac and Diabetes Risks	*Insulin*
Hot Flashes	*Progesterone, Estrogen*

Impaired Immune System	*DHEA, Anti-Oxidants*
Menopause and Menopausal Symptoms	*Progesterone, Estrogen, Testosterone, Thyroid, DHEA, Melatonin, Pregnenolone, Insulin, Growth Hormone*
Mood Changes (Depression, Anxiety, Irritability Panic Attacks, Mood Swings, Loss of Confidence)	*Progesterone, Testosterone, Thyroid, Serotonin, B-12, B-6, Iodine, Zinc, Selenium*
Sexual Function Problems, Loss of Desire, Vaginal Dryness	*Testosterone, Estrogen, Thyroid, DHEA, Iodine, Zinc, Selenium*
Skin Aging (Appearance of Wrinkles, Discoloration, Skin Dryness, Acne)	*Estrogen, Thyroid, DHEA, Growth Hormone, Vitamin C, Vitamin E, Amino-Peptides, Anti-Oxidants*
Sleep Disturbances (Diminished or Lighter Sleep)	*Progesterone, Thyroid, Melatonin, Iodine, Zinc, Selenium*

Sugar Cravings and Glucose Swings	*Insulin*
Urine Incontinence and Infections	*Estrogen*
Weight Gain	*Progesterone, Estrogen, Thyroid, Insulin, Nutrients that activate fat breakdown, Iodine, Zinc, Selenium*

Hormones begin to decrease around the age of thirty, and they continue to decrease as the years go on—up to a 50% decline by the age of fifty. Typically, however, most women don't *feel* the changes that these decreases and imbalances cause until they reach their forties or fifties. Some relate all of these symptoms to menopause. However, most experience these symptoms long before they reach a true state of menopause. As a result the symptoms are often ignored or misinterpreted. Because women feel that they are too young to be menopausal, they simply continue to feel *funky* until they reach a point where they are overwhelmed by their symptoms.

But women don't have to live with these symptoms. Though initially they may try to ignore or rationalize that they are *over forty* and the changes they are experiencing in their bodies are *normal*, it doesn't *have* to be *normal!* Once a woman is more informed as to the *causes* of these changes, the more she realizes that she doesn't have to live with them. Today a woman can safely correct the deficiencies of both hormones and nutrients. She can re-establish a healthy balance in order to achieve a more optimal state, resulting in her feeling better!

At this time there are three questions to ask yourself:

1) Do I want my state of hormones and nutrients at a *normal* level for a forty-year-old woman or an *optimal* level for a forty-year-old woman?
2) How old would I think I am if I didn't know how old I was?
3) How old would I like to feel regardless of my age?

Though you can't turn back the clock twenty years, there are things you can do to make you look and feel fabulous at any age, and it all starts from within.

Chapter Two: The Emotional Funk of the Brain

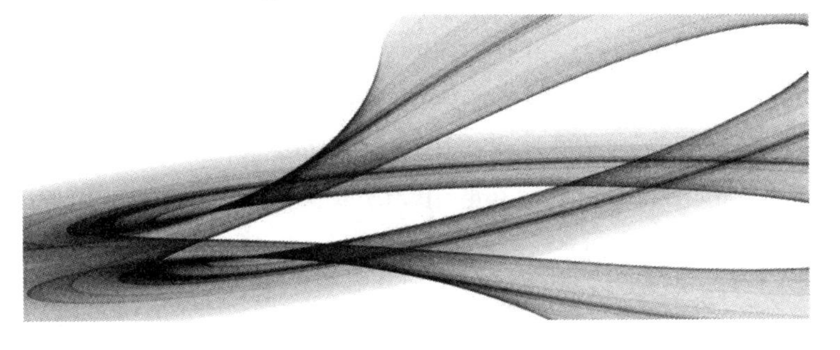

"What is necessary to change a person is to change his awareness of himself."
Abraham Maslow

After leaving the doctor's office, Lumi walked down 7th Avenue to the lab where she was to get her blood work done. Very few people were waiting, and she was in and out in no time. As she pulled her sleeve over her elbow to cover the band-aid on her arm, her stomach reminded her that she hadn't eaten breakfast yet. She began to walk back toward her car, but the smells of coffee and fresh baked cinnamon rolls filled the air and insisted that she not go any farther. She decided to pop into Charlotte's Coffee House and grab a quick bite to eat. The bells on the door jingled to announce her arrival as she entered the cheery shop. A round rosy-faced woman looked up from the counter and smiled at her. “Sit anywhere you want, Hon,” she called out. Lumi saw a small, obscure table for two in the back corner and worked her way to it.

She sat down and took quick note of all of the people having their breakfasts. Lumi always felt uncomfortable sitting by herself in a restaurant so she reached quickly into her handbag and pulled out a never-ending list of errands that she kept with her at all times and pretended to read it intently to look as though she was doing something of importance. She was interrupted by the same rosy-faced woman whose chubby hands handed her a menu.

“Coffee, Hon?” she asked.

Lumi nodded affirmatively and watched as the dark liquid filled her cup. Quickly scanning the menu she decided on scrambled eggs, dry wheat toast and fresh fruit. She placed her order and got back to her list.

It didn’t take long before her meal was placed in front of her. “Enjoy!” the rosy-faced woman said with a smile as she flipped her large hips, immediately turned and headed back to the coffee counter. Lumi looked down at her plate to find scrambled eggs, butter-soaked white toast and bacon. Lumi didn’t eat red meat, so this greasy piece of pig was a huge intrusion upon her plate. She tried to get the waitress’ attention to no avail, so figured she would attempt to enjoy the eggs that hadn’t soaked up the bacon grease and the bits of toast that weren’t dripping with butter. It wasn't what she ordered. She really wanted some fruit, but she decided to suck it up and just eat what she could.

She wasn't exactly sure where her inferiority complex came from, but she had one. Maybe she developed it after her divorce. Either way she didn't know why she felt so undeserving of having what she wanted, but the fact was she did. She didn't understand these feelings at all because it seemed that she never really had them before. Lately they had been overwhelming.

She didn't know why she felt so undeserving of having what she wanted, but the fact was she did.

It wasn't that she didn't have good things in her life. She had two wonderful children who made her happy and proud. Kyle and Kara were twins, age 20, who were both away at college. They were smart, driven, positive and respectful. Lumi, however, was facing the fact that her *babies* were grown up. Her children had less need for her participation, guidance or time at this point. She was adjusting to an empty nest and trying to figure out what her place and purpose was in life without the children at home. She realized that many women go through an identity crisis during this period, questioning whether they should have pursued careers or done something differently. Lumi even wondered, *what now?* as she tried to figure out what her life would be like going forward.

She felt tears well up in her eyes once again but fought to hold them off. Her self-esteem had sunk to a new low lately, and she attributed it to the fact that her body no longer looked the way it used to and that she didn't seem to have any purpose in life. Her moods fluctuated more, and she found herself on either a steep emotional slope sliding down quickly or on an emotional roller-coaster with no exit or off-button. Though she knew she had a lot to be thankful for, this emotional funk was beginning to drive her crazy and take control of her life. It just wouldn't go away. She had moments of happiness and contentment, but they didn't last. Something would always jolt her out of it and back to feeling insecure, inferior and unhappy or sad.

She admitted to herself that she felt depressed, so she tried hard to focus on something that her father taught her years ago. He always said that *one of the greatest gifts we are given is our mind, the ability to use it, and the power to choose our thoughts, our actions and our future.* Unfortunately, as Lumi grew older, she forgot what it was like to be able to do this.

One of the greatest gifts we are given is our mind, the ability to use it, and the power to choose our thoughts, our actions and our future.

She thought back to her conversation with Dr. Vida, who had discussed decreasing and fluctuating levels of hormones and nutrients in women's bodies and how they begin to have an adverse affect on the neurotransmitters in their brains. She learned that neurotransmitters transfer messages from nerve cells (neurons) to chemical impulses, back to electrical impulses from one cell to another. When nutrients or hormones are not at optimal levels, these neurotransmitters are not stimulated properly and don't function as they should, which can cause neurotransmitter disorders. As a result, the messages our minds receive often turn to a more depressive state. The effects of hormones have a huge impact on these neurotransmitters and how they relate to the mood center of our brains. A large portion of depressive symptoms can be attributed to these imbalances.

Lumi now saw herself as a different person than she had even a few years ago. She feared age was setting in and that time was running out. Emotions ran high and she wanted to feel young, vibrant, beautiful and happy again. She wanted to feel *good!* She wanted to have a purpose in life, and she wanted to feel like *somebody!*

What Lumi didn't know was that women often refer to this set of feelings as the *forty-funk.* Often after the age of forty, women begin to re-assess their lives, their careers and day-to-day activities, as well as their marriages. The divorce rate for women forty and over is 40% higher than any other age group. While not everyone experiences severe or all symptoms of the *forty-funk*, Lumi felt she did on many levels.

She pulled from her bag a second handout from Dr. Vida. Her eyes ran down the list of the emotional side-effects of unbalanced and decreased hormones and nutrients. She saw:

- Feelings of sadness, anxiousness or emptiness.
- Changes in sleep patterns with either sleeping too much or too little.
- Changes in eating patterns with reduced appetites and weight loss or increased appetites and weight gain.
- Irritability, restlessness or increased anger.
- Difficulty concentrating or making decisions.
- Lack of energy or fatigue and feelings of low energy.
- Feelings of worthlessness or hopelessness.
- Loss of interest in activities once enjoyed.
- Loss of interest in sexual activities.
- Persistent physical symptoms such as headaches, digestive issues or pain.
- Mood fluctuations.
- Physical changes in the exterior look of the body.

She quickly related to other symptoms listed. She knew that she lost her train of thought more often these days, sometimes forgetting why she went into a room. She often felt foggy-brained and wasn't able to concentrate well. Sometimes she would forget appointments, people's names or places, or even what she was about to say. She definitely felt as though she blanked out more often and would often think to herself, *where did I just go?* Though she laughed at herself on the occasions when she would put the milk in the cupboard instead of the refrigerator, she knew she was distracted and it was all so depressing.

The good news was that she now knew she wasn't the only woman experiencing these funky changes. *Maybe I'm not going crazy after all,* she thought. *I know I'm not happy now, but I guess if I want to change that, then I have to start taking responsibility for my life, my body and my mind. With Dr. Vida's help, maybe there is hope.* Feeling slightly encouraged, she paid the bill for her breakfast and exited without anyone noticing.

Illumination

The *forty-funk* can be a difficult time for a woman. Especially if she feels she has no control and only one option—to continue on the path she is on, let aging take its course, give up control of her body, and accept this as her lot in life.

Along with all of the physical changes she sees and experiences, the emotional roller-coaster she is on can be the most overwhelming. To dismiss these changes and feelings is very unhealthy because they are *real.* Low levels of energy are *real.* Not being able to sleep is *real.* Lack of sexual drive is *real.* Mood swings and emotional ups and downs are *real.* Depression is *real.* And feelings of confusion, forgetfulness and unhappiness are also *real.*

To consider whether hormones and nutrients are the culprits for a less-than-optimal state of mind, ask yourself these questions:

Do I find it harder to concentrate lately?

Do I get depressed more easily?

Do my moods fluctuate irrationally?

Is my libido lower than normal?

Do I have anxiety attacks now?

Has my mental sharpness declined?

Do I forget things more easily?

Do I have a hard time concentrating?

Do I have less energy than usual?

Do I want to sleep more than normal?

If you answered *yes* to more than a couple of these questions, you may have less-than-optimal levels of hormones and nutrients at the root of the problem. It could also be more serious than this. Either way, living this way and continuing to feel this way shouldn't be an option. The only acceptable option for you should be to take all the steps you can possibly take to find out the true causes for these mental changes. There should be no need for you to *not* feel good physically and mentally, to *not* feel good about your life, and to *not* feel good about yourself as a human being.

There should be no need for you to not feel good physically and mentally, to not feel good about your life, and to not feel good about yourself as a human being.

The good news is that there *are* such steps you can take to help you feel good once again without having to change your life dramatically. You don't have to have plastic surgery, get a divorce, sell all your assets and travel the world or join a commune. You may *choose* to do one or more of these things, but it will be totally up to you; and you will be making these choices with a healthy, cognitive mind and body.

The first step is for you to acknowledge that there are definitely changes taking place within (*and to*) your body and mind. These changes are not imagined. Once there is acknowledgement that these changes are real, awareness can take place as to the reasons for these changes. Once causes are identified and verified by a medical professional, you can make informed decisions to take whatever steps are necessary in order to decrease the effects of, or eliminate, the *forty-funk.*

When you do this, you will be taking the first step toward *Feeling Funkabulous*. Ask around and get recommendations for physicians who test hormone and nutrient levels.

Chapter Three: Telling the Funk to Take a Hike

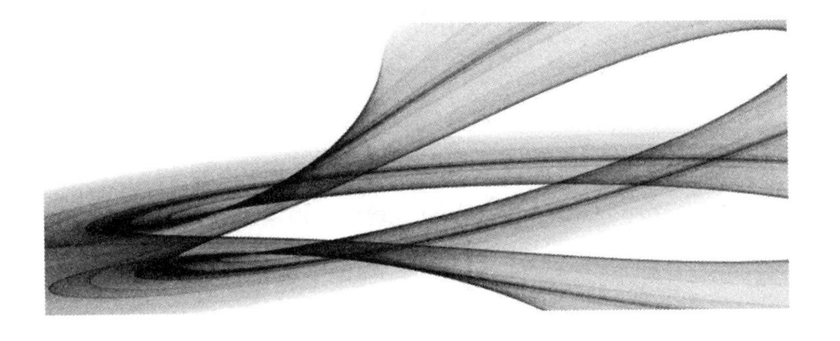

"There's nothing worse than being an aging young person."
Richard Pryor

Within two days after Lumi's first visit to Dr. Vida the lab results were received, and Dr. Vida detailed a three-step process to help dissipate Lumi's *forty-funk*. The first step entailed a prescription for hormone replacement therapy. Lumi, however, was hesitant because she had read numerous articles stating how harmful synthetic hormone replacement was for women. It was often made from horse urine and proved to be harmful in more ways than beneficial. She'd read stories of heart disease and cancer and became concerned about starting such a regimen. Yet, Dr. Vida explained that synthetic hormones would not be used or recommended. Instead she was recommending bio-identical hormones.

"Bio-identical hormones," Dr. Vida explained, "are exactly identical in molecular structure to the hormones that are made in the body. In fact, they are so identical to what the body produces that the body actually recognizes them as their own natural hormones. Synthetic hormones are not recognized as your own and stay in the body as toxins and carcinogens."

> *Bio-identical hormones are exactly identical in molecular structure to the hormones that are made in the body.*

She continued to alleviate Lumi's fears that bio-identical hormones would not cause breast cancer or heart disease. She was told that bio-identical hormones actually protect *against* such diseases, as well as aid in combating osteoporosis, high cholesterol, and mental decline.

The more Dr. Vida and Lumi spoke, the more questions Lumi had. "Please don't think I'm stupid," Lumi said, "but I thought hormone replacement therapy was only for women who were going through menopause, and I don't think I'm menopausal."

Dr. Vida reassured her that bio-identical hormone replacement was to be used before, during and after menopause. The woman's age didn't matter. It was simply the fact that the body was no longer producing hormones at optimal levels.

So Lumi used her bio-identical hormones religiously for the next two weeks. She rubbed her white cream onto her thighs and inner arms each morning and continued to research the effects of doing so on the Internet. She was amazed to find that this simple cream could protect bones, muscles, the heart and brain, as well as reduce depression, fatigue, irritability, anxiety, and memory and concentration loss. It could also help prevent weight gain! *If that's the case*, she thought, *I'll keep using it!*

Diminished hormones, however, was not Lumi's only problem. Her blood work also showed that her thyroid levels were low, as were other necessary nutrients. Dr. Vida explained that vitamins are very important to a healthy body because every hormone needs a vitamin or mineral to activate it. For example, B-vitamins help activate estrogen production; and selenium, zinc and iodine help the thyroid. Lumi would need to add some specific supplements to her diet in order to boost those levels. She

Vitamins are very important to a healthy body because every hormone needs a vitamin or mineral to activate it.

would also begin a low dose of thyroid medicine (T3 – T4) to help increase her thyroid function.

At this point Lumi could actually begin to see the connection. If her iodine levels were low, her thyroid might not produce at optimal levels, which could lead to additional weight gain. If her B-Vitamin levels were low, her production of estrogen might decrease, which could cause a whole host of symptoms that she had been experiencing. She was beginning to fully understand the *cause* of the symptoms she was enduring. She was also beginning to get excited that the adjustments that Dr. Vida was making would actually make a difference.

Finally Dr. Vida recommended a week of detoxification—cleansing the body of toxins. Lumi recalled their conversation.

"Toxins?" she questioned.

Dr. Vida smiled, "We are exposed to toxins daily—from cell phones and computers to plastics and preservatives. There are toxins in our food, our water, and our air. When toxins are present, hormones and nutrients don't absorb into the body as they should."

When toxins are present, nutrients can't be absorbed in the body. When the amount of nutrients being absorbed by the body isn't sufficient, hormones can't be produced at the levels necessary.

"Okay," Lumi repeated, "when toxins are present, nutrients (or what I call vitamins) can't be absorbed in the body. When the amount of nutrients being absorbed by the body isn't sufficient, hormones can't be produced at the levels necessary. When hormones aren't produced at optimal levels, then your body begins to experience everything that I've been experiencing!"

Dr. Vida nodded, "I think you've got it! In addition, many physicians believe that good health begins in the intestines. When the environment in the intestines is not in healthy order, it can affect every cell in your body. The greatest challenge our bodies face is the successful removal of wastes and toxins. Then she explained the simple process of detoxification, which would require Lumi to eat nothing but vegetables, drink lots of purified water and add a cleansing product for a period of one week. "This will clean the toxins out of your intestines and jump-start your metabolism."

With the help of Dr. Vida's three-step process of hormone replacement, nutrient supplementation and detoxification, Lumi was beginning to correct a lot of the *physical* causes of the *forty-funk.* Two weeks from Lumi's first consultation with Dr. Vida she had lost five pounds, her skin and hair looked and felt better, she was sleeping more soundly, and she wasn't quite as moody. She also actually had thoughts of sex now and then, which she hadn't for quite some time. For the first time in a long time she felt encouraged that there might actually be a light at the end of the tunnel she had been in for the past year.

Illumination

There is a simple path a woman can take to begin to help restore her body and slow down the effects of aging. Yet more than that, three simple steps of hormone replacement, nutrient supplementation and detoxification can help to reduce or eliminate those nasty side effects that a woman endures as she gets older.

Every woman's goal should be to live her life better each day than the last. A woman stands at a precipice during this period in her life. Will she simply accept that it is there, give in to it and then fall slowly to her death? Or will she take action, grow wings and soar to a better place? With today's knowledge about what happens to a woman's body physically, there are no excuses for giving up and accepting the so-called fate of experiencing the *forty-funk*. A woman has the ability to slow down her biological clock, correct the deficiencies that are taking place within her body and feel better than she ever has.

Dr. Sangeta Pati, MD, FACOG, of Orlando, Florida, is recognized by physicians nationally and internationally as an authority in the field of anti-aging and hormone replacement therapy. She has summarized below some of the basics of restoring hormones, restoring nutrients and removing toxins in order to give you a base of knowledge in which to begin.

RESTORING HORMONES

What Are Bio-Identical Hormones?

Bio-identical hormones are rapidly becoming popular among women who do not want to suffer the symptoms of physical or mental aging anymore. The body does not know the difference between the hormone it makes and bio-identical hormones, because they are exactly identical in molecular structure to the hormones which are made in the body. They are compounded from yam and soy by removing and adding extra molecules so they are recognized by your cells and tissues as your own. Synthetic hormones have extra molecules that are not recognized by the body. They are not broken down by our body's enzymes, and they may stay in the body for long periods of time as toxins and carcinogens.

How Are They Used?

Bio-identical hormones are compounded by prescription only. Healthcare providers evaluate hormone requirements through clinical symptoms, and possibly, blood or saliva tests. The prescription is tailored to the exact amount of each hormone needed for the individual's balance. Hormones that are initially evaluated for replacement include the three estrogens (estrone, estradiol, estriol), progesterone and testosterone. These can be taken orally, by patch or as a cream. Additional hormones that should be considered include melatonin, DHEA, thyroid hormone and growth hormone.

What Are the Benefits?

Bio-identical hormone replacement will significantly reduce symptoms associated with hormonal decline *before, during* and *after* menopause including hot flashes, vaginal dryness, skin thinning, memory loss, concentration loss, anxiety, depression, weight gain, irritability, fatigue, insomnia, decreased sex drive, urine loss, muscle weakness and joint pain. In addition to symptom relief, bio-identical hormones protect your brain, heart, vessels, bones, skin, hair follicles and muscles from decline. Most women who start on bio-identical hormones feel emotionally and physically better within two weeks.

What Is The Data?

So far there is more data on synthetic hormones than bio-identical hormones because synthetic hormones are patented and drug companies pay for the studies. Bio-identical hormones are generic to the human body like vitamins. They cannot be patented and therefore, drug companies have not yet been interested in footing the bill. We do know that bio-identical hormones have been used in Europe for over 60 years and studies show that they are both safe and effective. They have been shown to protect against heart disease, high cholesterol, osteoporosis, and mental decline. They do not increase the risk of breast cancer, and, in fact, there is data showing that they may protect *against* breast cancer. At precise doses that exactly replace your body's deficiency, there are no known side effects. They have the exact same action on the body as one's own hormones.

Should You Take Them?

Some ask: "Am I safe taking hormones?" I ask how safe are you *without* your hormones? The cells in your brain, heart, vessels, bones, skin, hair follicles and muscles all have receptors for hormones. As the hormone levels dwindle, all these cells and tissues lose stimulation, leading to a rapid decline and advance of degenerative diseases. If you would correct a vitamin or mineral deficiency with bio-identical vitamin or mineral replacement, you should consider replacing a declining hormone.

RESTORING NUTRIENTS

Every cell reaction produces damaging free radicals that require anti-oxidants to neutralize them. Every cell reaction, whether to activate a brain chemical, produce energy, or to break down fat and build muscle, needs a vitamin or mineral to proceed. Every hormone needs a vitamin and mineral to activate its receptor. As an example:

- Thyroid hormone needs zinc, selenium and iodine to be activated.
- Insulin needs chromium, vanadium, magnesium and Vitamin B3
- And estrogen needs B vitamins and cobalt.

Although in the United States we are daily bombarded by the concepts of anti-oxidants, bad carbs, good carbs, mindful eating, transfats, good fats and low fats, as a nation we are mineral-deficient. The leaching of the soil leads to a state of relative nutrient depletion in our food supply. We can improve our food-based nutrition by eating more vegetables, eating organic produce, increasing good fats and avoiding preservatives, processed food, simple sugars and bad fats; but we cannot get the level of nutrients needed to activate hormones, energy cycles, brain chemistries and other pathways through food alone. This is the premise for supplementing nutrients through superfoods and formulated products.

REMOVING TOXINS

Compared to most other developed countries we are exposed to fifty times the level of toxins through water, air, industry, computers, cell phones, preservatives, plastics and fumes. These toxins reside in the bowel, the liver and the fat tissues. Toxins increase the acidity in the body which impairs all chemical reactions, which normally proceed at pH 7.0 and above. As an example:

- Bowel toxins like Candida or other bacterial overgrowth impair absorption of nutrients.
- Low oxygen, due to shallow breathing, produces acidity.
- Electromagnetic radiation from cell phones and computers work at energetic levels to impair chemical function and immunity.
- Liver toxins impair the detoxification process that occurs in the liver.
- Viruses, fungi and parasites are present everywhere and accumulate in the body.
- Heavy metals diminish neurological functions, among other things.

Toxins impair the absorption and utilization of nutrients and hormones. This is the premise for regular bowel, liver and tissue detoxification and specific detoxification as needed (1).

With the life expectancy of women getting longer and longer, a woman currently age forty could conceivably be looking forward to living another forty to sixty years! On average women will live until they are around eighty years old, and it's possible that some will live until they are one hundred. Some Japanese Okinawans live to the age of one hundred and twenty today in a healthful manner! If that's the case, why doesn't every woman slow the aging process down and work toward feeling better each day than the last? She simply needs to live each year as youthfully and healthfully (both physically and mentally) as she can. To do that, she will need to consider giving herself a gift and seeking out a medical professional that practices the three steps of anti-aging: bio-identical hormonal replacement, nutritional assessment and restoration and detoxification of the body. This first step toward being *Funkabulous* could be one of the greatest gifts a woman gives to herself.

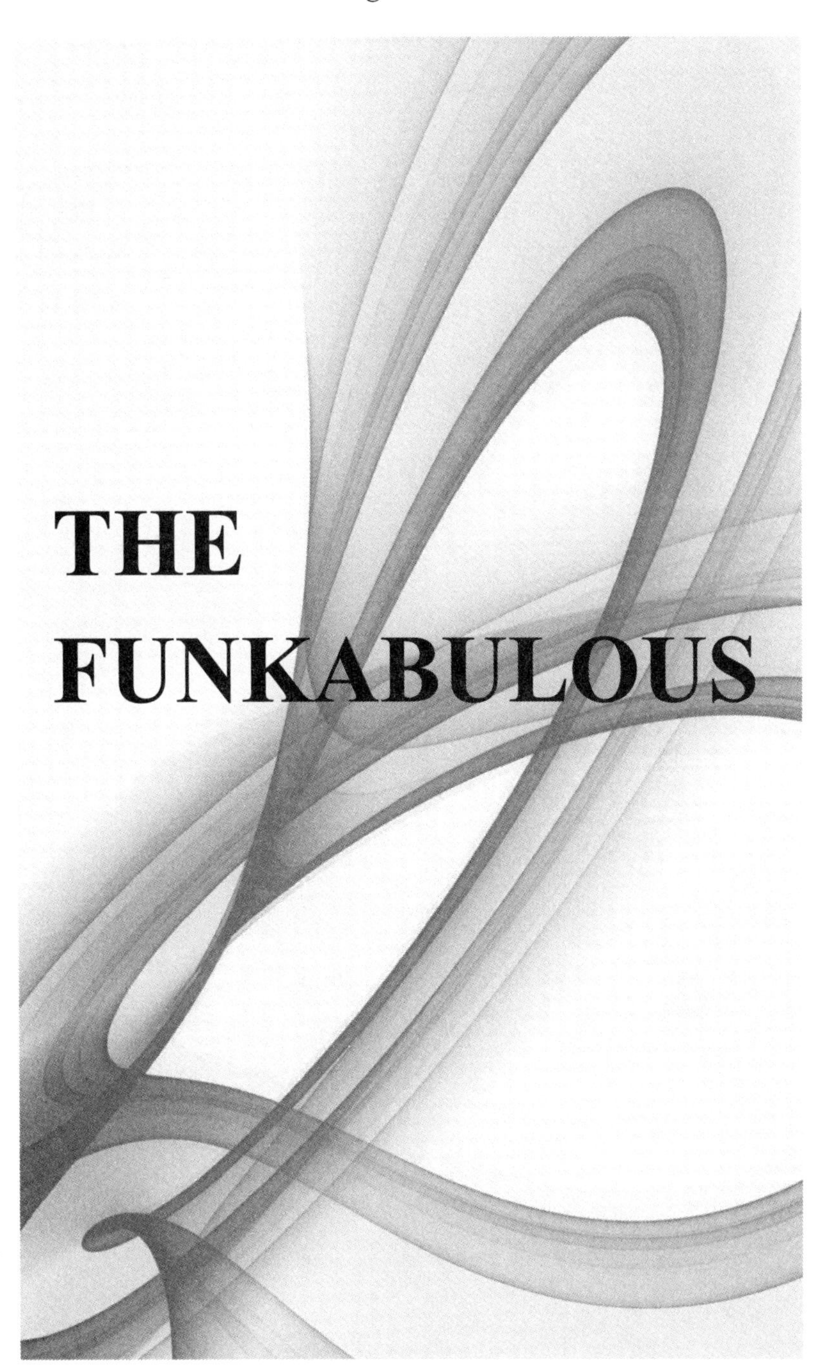
THE
FUNKABULOUS

Chapter Four: Reflections and Belief

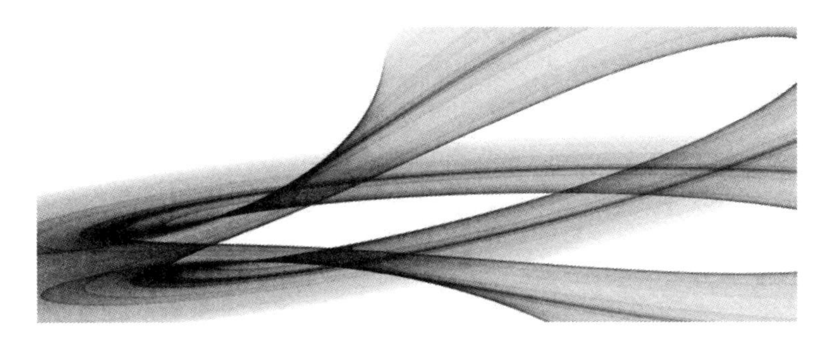

"Life is like a mirror. If you frown at it, it frowns back. If you smile at it, it returns the greeting."
Herbert Samuels

It had now been three months since her first visit to Dr. Vida. Lumi was looking better and physically feeling better, but her thoughts were still filled with comments that supported a lack of confidence, low self-esteem and depreciating beliefs about her looks, attributes and abilities. To her, it didn't matter how much better she got physically if she couldn't see it or feel happy about it.

One Wednesday morning Lumi began her day in her typical manner, yet on this particular day she noticed she had a little more energy and a little more enthusiasm. She found her keys quite quickly, had another to-do list of errands in her bag and was headed once again to 7th Avenue.

As she drove toward the highway, she could see that cars were lined up and stopped. She knew there was most likely an accident that would probably tie up traffic for hours. So she decided to take a back route she hadn't driven in years. As she drove through the neighborhoods she was saddened to see how rundown and messy they had become. Houses were unpainted, weeds grew where grass once was, remnants of furniture and appliances filled many yards, and garbage lined the streets. *It's only been a few years,* she thought. *How could things have changed so much in such a short period of time?*

She pulled up slowly to a stop sign. As she scanned the unsightly view ahead of her she was startled by a man who tapped on the side of her car with his hand to get her attention. He leaned into her open passenger window and reached his dirty hand toward her as he asked if she could help him out. The pungent odor of sweat and alcohol sent her heart racing. With trembling hands she quickly grabbed a few stray dollars that had been shoved into her handbag and gingerly held them toward him. "Thank you," he said as he backed away.

Lumi drove on, shaking, but feeling very sad for this man. She thought how his life might be different if he simply detoxed a bit. She looked at the neighborhood that no one took pride in, and thought it simply needed a good cleaning and for the trash to be hauled away. It, too, needed a good detoxification. Then she thought about how much she had changed over the past three months under Dr. Vida's guidance, but realized there was one area of her life that still needed detoxification as well.

I've come a long way from where I was, she thought, *but I still have another area of my life that needs detoxifying: my thinking. I've been cramming my mind with negative and harmful thoughts. No wonder I couldn't focus on positive thoughts that could have helped me through this difficult time. How does that saying go? Garbage in; garbage out? I was putting in a lot of garbage, and that was all that was coming out! There are still some bags to get rid of. How do I do that? I detoxed my body. How do I detox my mind?*

I detoxed my body. How do I detox my mind?

Lumi had done a fair amount of reading in her life. She had learned that people who worry and process fearful and negative thoughts in their minds rationalize that they have adequate reason to believe them to be true and often expand and exaggerate them even more. Very few people exaggerate the *good* thoughts they hold, but for some reason negative thoughts are often expanded dramatically. Entire lives can be based on fear, worry and negativity, placing a dramatic amount of stress on the body. It is a prime example of garbage being fed to the brain. If this is all the mind receives, then that's all that will be expressed in the life. She wondered if she should tackle a little housekeeping in her brain and get rid of some of her mental garbage.

She wondered, *is it possible that all the negative thoughts I've been having about myself have multiplied the negativity and depression I was feeling? Am I my own worst enemy? Have I sabotaged my future with my negative thinking habits? Is it possible that this also has played a part in keeping me from my dream of writing a novel? Can I get rid of my mental trash? Can I change my mindset and detox my thoughts? Can I really write the book I dreamed of writing?*

Is it possible that all the negative thoughts I've been having about myself have multiplied the negativity and depression I was feeling?

Without answering herself, Lumi turned onto 7th Avenue and found a good parking space. Her first stop was a shop that had been in business for over fifteen years. The *Hangup's* specialty was mirrors, picture frames, plant hangers…anything that hangs on a wall. The proprietor, Rita, was an old friend of Lumi's from the days when they lived next to each other, raising their children at the same time. Lumi pushed open the door of the shop and the little bell tinkled a greeting. Rita came from the next aisle where she had been dusting the displayed items.

As soon as Rita saw who had entered the shop, she exclaimed loudly, "Lumi!" and moved toward her with outstretched arms and a big smile. Lumi smiled and embraced the vivacious redhead, truly glad to see her.

"How have you been?" Lumi quizzed.

"Hanging around and almost perfect!" Rita grinned. That was her standard answer whenever anyone asked her that question. Both women laughed lightly at the familiarity of the exchange. Rita was about ten years older than Lumi, and Lumi had always thought she looked like Agnes Morehead of *Bewitched*—especially with the red hair, confident attitude and quick wit.

"I'm looking for a new mirror for my front hall. I don't like the one hanging there anymore," Lumi stated.

"Okay then, let's see what we can find on the back wall display." The worn old wooden floor groaned comfortably beneath their feet as the two women exchanged news about their children and walked to the brick wall that was the back of the shop. There were several shapes and styles available that fit Lumi's requirements, but she enjoyed shopping for something new for her home, so she was in no hurry.

She began peering into the mirrors one by one, examining the quality of her image and the details of the frames. Wisely Rita hovered in the background and let her customer browse. But Rita loved to talk and it was hard for her to keep silent for very long. She could see that as Lumi looked at herself in the mirrors, she seemed to be struggling with something. She didn't smile, and there was a heaviness about her. Deciding Lumi needed to lighten up Rita turned to one of the mirrors, looked into it and let out a loud yell.

"DAMN! IT HAPPENED AGAIN!"

Lumi jumped in surprise. "What? What happened again?"

Rita looked into the mirror with a big smile and said, "I just got better looking than I was yesterday!"

As ridiculous as it was, Lumi couldn't help but laugh. Rita whispered a thank-you to the Universe and noticed that Lumi seemed a bit more relaxed than when she came in.

"Take a look at this one over here, Lumi," Rita suggested. "It's a nice oval shape that is flattering to everyone." Lumi obediently moved to the oval mirror and glanced at her reflection.

"THERE IT GOES AGAIN!" Rita exploded.

"WHAT?" Lumi yelled in surprise.

"You just got better looking, too!" Rita grinned widely as she moved next to Lumi and squeezed her arm. Lumi started laughing and Rita joined her. After a few minutes of shared silliness, Lumi's spirits lifted and she joked, "If that is all it takes to get me out of this funk, I'd better buy this oval mirror and look into it several times a day!"

Rita responded, "Don't buy the first one you see! Here, come look at this square one with the wooden frame. Lumi obliged, and while she was looking at the detail in the frame, Rita took advantage of the moment and said something she thought Lumi needed to hear.

"You know, you can see different things in different mirrors." Lumi looked at her skeptically. Rita persisted. "For instance, this round mirror is very special. It used to hang on my living room wall beside the front door. Every time I left the house I'd check my hair in this mirror before I opened the door. This is the mirror I talked to when I'd tell myself how great I looked and how happy everyone I met was going to be to see me again. Then I'd go out the door *expecting* to have good encounters with everyone. And that was what I got. This is also the mirror I told my deepest desire to when I was still working at the drug store. I'd look into this mirror and *see* myself owning my own shop someday. Now look at me! This mirror is my friend. This mirror is not for sale."

I like to give people a sense of how to really use mirrors to see themselves as they'd like to be, and how to visualize what they want in their future. And, you know, it really works!

"Then why isn't it at home instead of here?" Lumi asked.

"Because I like to give people a sense of how to *really* use mirrors to see themselves as they'd *like* to be, and how to visualize what they want in their future. And, you know, it really works! Go on, try it.

Look into that tall narrow mirror with the matte Florentine gold patina on the frame to your right and imagine yourself doing what you really wish you could do, whatever that is."

Lumi didn't have to think twice about what she wanted. She wanted it for over twenty years. She wanted to write her own book. Not just any book. A New York Times Best Seller was what she had in mind. She had lots of ideas and lots of background to draw from. She only lacked the belief that she could do it. Gingerly she told Rita her wish. Rita listened well, reading between the lines and feeling honored that her friend trusted her enough to share her dream. She sensed this was a big step for Lumi and she wanted to encourage without pushing harder than was necessary.

"That should be no problem with your background in journalism. How many years did you write magazine articles?"

"I was a staff writer for the largest newspaper in Boston when I was in my twenties. That gained me some national and even global attention because one of my stories was picked up by the Associated Press and was circulated all over the world. I remember the tingling in my soul when that happened. When I left the newspaper business, I wrote feature articles on many subjects for a very successful women's magazine in the Chicago area. When I had the twins twenty years ago, I was so busy with them I switched to free-lancing whenever I had time. Gradually I just stopped writing altogether and took on editing jobs for a couple of local magazines. I've never written a book, but I have so many scraps of paper with notes on them and so many ideas in my head for pulling them all together that I feel if I just put my fingers on my computer keys my book is going to come out!"

"Then start writing today!" Rita exclaimed as she threw her arms in the air. "As far as I can see, you only have one thing stopping you."

"What's that?" Lumi curiously asked.

"Believing you can do it and acting on that belief." Then Rita held her breath. Would Lumi take up the challenge she just proposed? Or would she revert to the limiting negative thought patterns that so far had kept her from fulfilling her dream?

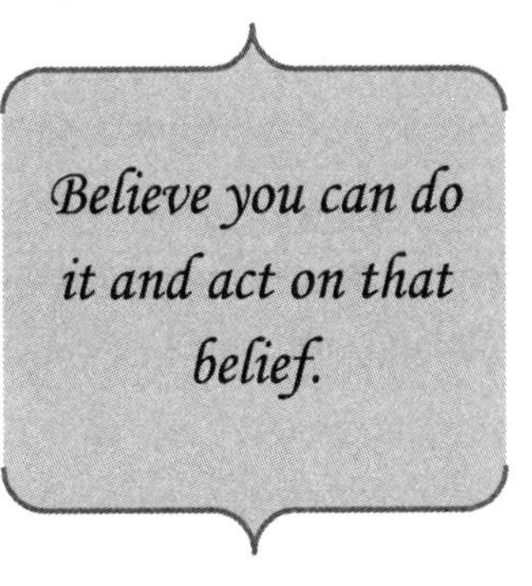

Lumi stared first at Rita's face smiling behind her in the mirror, then shifted her eyes to her own face in the same mirror. Still wearing a large smile, Rita stepped out of the range of vision, leaving Lumi looking only at herself. She wasn't thrilled with what she saw. When had she given up on herself? What had made her think she *couldn't* write when writing was all she had lived for years ago? Suddenly the answer was written all over her face.

Lumi had put her dreams aside when her mother became ill and she was consumed with the cares and responsibilities of taking care of her. After her mother's death, handling the financial aspects of her considerable estate became a full time job. She realized that she had lost her most encouraging advocate for her writing, along with her own desire to pursue it. But standing there looking at the lines on her face and the stray gray hairs on her head, she realized that during that time she made a choice to set her dreams aside. Later she realized that she stopped believing she was capable of achieving her dreams. Now she was faced with the question: Who said she couldn't at least make a start on writing that book of hers and move one step toward her dreams once again? *No one but me,* she realized with a stab of searing regret.

Standing just beside her and observing in the mirror the change coming over Lumi's face, Rita gently placed her hands on both of Lumi's shoulders and called Lumi's attention to the cathedral-window-type of point at the top of the mirror.

"Look at the top of the mirror, Lumi," Rita urged. "It's pointing *up.* The sky's the limit for you. Go for it!" she whispered in Lumi's left ear.

The sky's the limit for you. Go for it!

Lumi seemed to hesitate for a few seconds, but she was really rearranging her thinking to embrace a new idea. Suddenly she broke into a wide smile, reached up and squeezed both of Rita's hands as they rested on her shoulders. "I'll do that!" she said with a great burst of resolve she didn't know she possessed. "And I'll take *this* mirror, please. It's perfect for me and for the office of a soon-to-be author, and I swear that's what I'm going to be within one year. So let's find another mirror for my hallway."

Over the next hour Lumi looked at more mirrors than she ever thought she'd see in her lifetime. Whenever Lumi seemed especially interested in one, Rita asked her to envision something bigger in a different area of her life. From their long friendship Rita knew her friend liked to cook and entertain. She also knew she tended to put herself and her considerable talents down. So Rita pushed Lumi to think about how she would like to see her life change in different areas.

"You have to see this area of your life not the way it is, but the way you want it to be," Rita explained. "You have to clean out the bad thoughts in your mind, be grateful for all that you have in your life, eliminate the excuses that are holding you back, and replace them with positive thoughts, even if you don't believe them yet. (The operative word is *yet.*) Eventually you will believe them, and the more you say them, the deeper your belief will go. Call into existence what you *want* and not what you *have.* Continue to focus on the way you *want* your life to be, not how it is. Eventually the new positive thoughts will become your reality. This is the way the Universe works, Lumi. I know, because someone did this very same thing for me."

Call into existence what you want and not what you have. Continue to focus on the way you want your life to be, not how it is. Eventually the new positive thoughts will become your reality. This is the way the Universe works.

The exercise was both an eye-opener and a moment of truth for Lumi as Rita expertly encouraged her to set higher expectations and goals for herself. Both women were well aware of what was happening, and Lumi was grateful for the unsolicited help. She knew how much she needed it and she was more than ready for it.

An hour later Lumi and Rita carried not one, not two, but four carefully wrapped mirrors out to Lumi's car and laid them gently in the trunk. There was a small round one framed in brushed brass for the front hallway, just large enough to check her makeup and hair before leaving the house. There was a small shiny copper-framed one shaped like the sun for her sunny kitchen. Lumi loved copper and used it lavishly in her kitchen. The third mirror was framed in a simple ceramic white and would go on her patio across from the hummingbird feeder to multiply the joy of watching the birds. And, of course, there was the inspirational one she loved the most: the cathedral window-shaped one for her office.

They stood back and surveyed the trunk full of well-padded packages that signified a real break-through. Lumi smiled. Rita had gently guided her through a real catharsis of her soul as she listened and learned to think positively and to see herself not the way she was at that moment, but the way she *wanted* to be. Rita was surprised to learn that this woman had more than one passion. She not only yearned to write a book, she had other dreams and desires in other areas that had also lay dormant for the last dozen years or more.

Listen and learn to think positively and see yourself not the way you are at that moment, but the way you want to be.

For one, there was her love of cooking and entertaining friends. The copper and white ceramic mirrors would serve as reminders of her talents in those two areas and stir her up to new culinary heights. She would practice imagining it all happening just the way she wanted it to be.

The round mirror with the brushed brass frame for the front hallway would be her reminder as she left home to face the world that she was a valuable human being who had a lot to give. Every time she looked at it, she would read the little plaque she had ordered to hang under it; *Good Things are Going to Happen!*

Though Lumi was financially secure due to her mother's estate, she never spent much money on herself. She loved to buy abundantly for others, but could never justify in her mind spending on things *she* might want. The mirrors were her first big purchase in quite some time. While shopping for these, however, she also admitted her secret desire to completely redecorate her bedroom, complete with a Jacuzzi tub for two in the adjoining bath. Now she knew it was okay to have this desire, *and* that it would come to fruition in the near future. She was anxious to start making plans for it and felt worthy enough to spend the money on it.

Back at home and thinking about all her renewed hopes and goals for her future, Lumi realized she still had a lot of passion in her for the things she wanted from life. Thanks to Rita and her mirrors, she had no doubt she was going to have it all. But all that shopping and decision-making and cleaning out the cobwebs in her brain and replacing it with hope and plans had worn her out. Suddenly she was very sleepy, and for the first time in weeks she *expected* to get a good night's rest. She prepared the house for the night by almost completely closing the windows in case it rained. She yawned and then smiled. She couldn't remember the last time she yawned! The bio-identical hormones were working. She sensed the shift in her mental attitude was working, too, thanks to her friend Rita. She had goals and the intent to accomplish them. For the first time in a very long time it seemed that *everything* in her life was working! As she brushed her teeth just before getting into bed, she glanced at herself in the bathroom mirror on the door of the old medicine cabinet. *I'll have to go see Rita again tomorrow at The Hangup,* she thought. *I need a new mirror in here.*

Illumination

Two thousand years ago there lived a slave of the Roman Empire named Epictetus. He was released from slavery later in life and became a leading Greek scholar and philosopher on living one's life. He said, "We are disturbed not by events, but by the views which we take of them." How you see events in your mind is *your* reality. How others see the same event is *their* reality, though it may be totally different from how you saw it. Who is right? Both of you! The view you have of an event, regardless of its nature, becomes your belief of that event. No one can tell you differently.

> *How you see events in your mind is your reality. How others see the same event is their reality.*

Consider this scenario: Dee and Linda took their children to play at the park. Dee kept a watchful eye over the children for fear of strangers and to keep them from hurting themselves on the play equipment. Linda had a more relaxed attitude and sat chatting to Dee, not worrying or watching the children as intently. At home that evening Dee complained to her husband about how stressful a day she had spent taking the children to the park. "There were all kinds of strange people there, and I had to watch *all* the children because Linda wasn't watching them. I don't think it's a safe environment, and it's not a good place to take them."

When asked about her day, Linda had a different view. "It was wonderful! I was able to go to the park, sit in the sunshine and chat with a friend. The children had a great time playing, and they enjoyed every minute on the playground. It was a wonderful day!" Linda and Dee saw the same events differently.

Tony Robbins, author and lecturer, states, "You see, it's never the environment; it's never the events of our lives, but the meaning we attach to the events—how we interpret them—that shapes who we are today and who we will become tomorrow" (2).

When the brain is being bombarded by negative chatter such as fear, worry or negativity, a person's outer world reflects it. But what about the negative chatter of feelings of guilt, shame, self-pity, anger, embarrassment, resentfulness, powerlessness, discouragement, loneliness, self-condemnation, low self-image and poor self-esteem? Everyone has experienced some of these feelings. Yet during this stage in a woman's life, as the *forty-funk* starts to set in, she tends to have more and more of these negative, self-defeating feelings. Then:

- She tends to gang up on herself and dig deep to find all that she can possibly find that she thinks is *wrong* with her. She focuses on that.

- She compares herself to others.

- She looks for ways she doesn't measure up.

- She feels guilty for not being super-mom.

- She thinks she isn't talented enough to start a new career.

- She thinks she is overweight and no longer attractive.

- She feels she just doesn't measure up!

She gives all those negative thoughts priority in her brain; and as a result, her actions and beliefs reflect those thoughts. If a woman isn't careful, she can begin a downward spiral that can end in low self-esteem, having no belief in herself and unhappiness. *As you believe, so you achieve.* How a woman sees herself and believes herself to be *is* what she becomes.

How a woman sees herself and believes herself to be is what she becomes.

Even if a woman were to set aside all of her thoughts for a moment and forget about the results of her thinking, she would still have to face the physical ramifications of negative chatter in her brain. Negative thoughts, regardless of what they are, disrupt the body's entire energy system, increase free radicals and compromise the immune system. This can create an increase in cholesterol, raise blood pressure and cause heart disease, strokes and cancers. Then, circulation, the heart and the entire nervous system is affected. Thoughts such as these stress the body, age a person prematurely and are poisonous to one's health. Research has found that *emotional* health is the catalyst to *physical* health.

Research has found that emotional health is the catalyst to physical health.

According to Deepak Chopra, a physician and author on mind-body wellness, "The way you think and the way you behave can influence your lifespan by 30 to 50 years." Positive emotions can improve physical health and negative emotions can obviously impair it (3).

Positive emotions can improve physical health and negative emotions can impair it.

So what is a person to do? Epictetus states, "There is only one way to happiness, and that is to cease worrying about things which are beyond the power of our will." Worrisome, fearful and negative thinking will eat away at a person both mentally and physically over time. Suffering from these thoughts is optional, and it is not a good option! Choose another option: to cleanse and detoxify one's mind of all of these harmful thoughts.

Whenever a negative thought pops into your head, replace it with a new, positive, uplifting thought.

Detoxifying the brain is the first mental step toward feeling fabulous. Whenever a negative thought pops into your head, think of your brain as a separate entity (possibly that crabby old aunt that no one can stand!) You may *hear* what she says to you, but you don't have to *listen* to it! Stop yourself. Say, "Thank you for your comment, but I choose to think something else." Then replace the original thought with a new, positive, uplifting thought. Take control of your thoughts. Don't let your thoughts control you. Once you replace negative thoughts with positive ones, you'll start seeing positive results.

Suppose you are getting ready to go out for dinner with friends one evening, and you look in the mirror and think, *I'm fat and I look horrible!* Recognize that this thought is in your head. Stop yourself, even say, ***"STOP!"*** out loud. You might choose to say, "Thank you, Aunt Crabby, but I think…." Then replace that thought with another. Find something—anything—even one thing that is good about how you look. "My dress is blue, and I always get compliments when I wear this color. My eyes look beautiful tonight. I love my new haircut," or anything you can find that is positive.

At first this may be a bit difficult, but it gets easier and easier with practice. In fact, soon you can make it even more fun. As negative thoughts pop into your head, don't only counter them with something positive, but try countering them with something totally outrageous that makes you smile and laugh! As you look in the mirror, say as Austin Powers, from the movie, *Austin Powers: International Man of Mystery*, might say, *"I'm gorgeous Baby!"* then wink at yourself or lick your finger, touch your behind, and make a sizzling noise because you are so hot!

When you get up in the morning and drag yourself into the bathroom, go right to the mirror! (Okay… I know. You're probably thinking *the goal is to feel BETTER about myself, not WORSE, so why do I want to look at myself at my worst possible time of the day!*) Trust me. Take a look, and then say with as much enthusiasm as you can, ***"WOW, you're BEAUTIFUL! You're PERFECT! You get better looking every day!"*** It has to make you laugh. It's not a pretty sight! But the strange thing that happens is that this tends to set the whole tone for the day. As negative thoughts begin to creep in throughout the day, you can go quickly to the mirror and repeat this statement, or counter it with something a little more positive.

WOW, you're BEAUTIFUL! You're PERFECT! You get better looking every day!

Maybe you are feeling purposeless or worthless, or that you aren't as smart as other women, or aren't needed by your children anymore. First, you must recognize that you are having these thoughts. Then it is *crucial* to take control of these thoughts. Don't give these negative thoughts power. Defend yourself IMMEDIATELY with a positive, reaffirming thought. Ask yourself, *if the negative things I was thinking were said about my best friend, how would I respond?* Most likely you would come to the defense of your best friend and defend him or her adamantly. You need to defend yourself just as

Don't let anyone—especially you—say anything negative about you!

forcefully. Don't let anyone—especially you—say anything negative about you!

Detoxifying the brain doesn't happen overnight, however. You can't expect to do it once and think that you have eliminated all the garbage that you have accumulated over the past years. Unfortunately it's not like taking a big dose of Metamucil. It's a process. It's a lifestyle. It's something that you may do several times a day depending on how much trash you need to take out. Initially you could be running to the curb with your trash can full of negative thoughts every few minutes. But eventually you won't need to make so many trips. As more positive, reaffirming thoughts replace the destructive, negative ones, you will find that soon your brain is cleansed. Then like anything else, it will simply be on a maintenance schedule: Clean as needed!

Chapter Five: Gratefulness

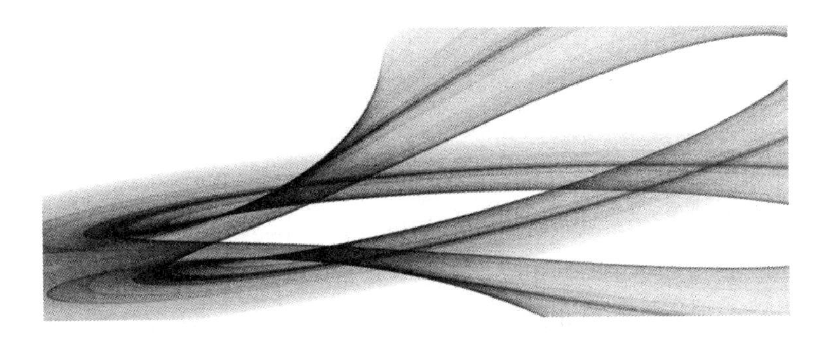

"Whatever we are waiting for—peace of mind, contentment, grace, the inner awareness of simple abundance—it will surely come to us, but only when we are ready to receive it with an open and grateful heart."
Sarah Ban Breathnach

The next morning Lumi woke up feeling different than she had been accustomed to as soon as she opened her eyes. For some inexplicable reason she felt lighter, in her spirit and in her body. She wondered about it until she remembered what an extraordinary day she experienced yesterday. She threw back the covers and swung her feet to the floor in one fluid motion and hit the ground running—literally. She trotted into the kitchen. *Still there*, she thought. Checking the patio she grinned. *Still the same.*

The office, front hall and bedroom revealed the same. All were still there the same as she left them the night before. All four mirrors were hanging where they were supposed to be. She had, indeed, spent a small fortune on mirrors yesterday but she wasn't one bit remorseful. She dropped back onto the bed, smiled and breathed deeply. This was not the way she had been starting her days during the last few years! It felt better than good. It felt *fabulous.* She thought about her upcoming day. Since she hadn't finished her list of errands on 7th Avenue yesterday, her plan was to return there today and take care of the rest of them. She laughed out loud and thought, *I didn't get everything on my list done, but I wouldn't have missed the mirror lesson for anything!*

A few hours later Lumi arrived on 7th Avenue and decided to park in the first parking space she came across. Though she was headed to the optical store at the end of the street, she thought it would be a beautiful day to walk a bit and consider it *getting a little exercise!* She admitted she really enjoyed walking down The Avenue (as she called it). For some reason there was no other street named *avenue* in this town… only 7th Avenue. One explanation was that originally there had only been seven streets in this small town, and this one was the widest of all, with the other six all narrower and less populated. In the town's early days all of the original merchants chose to open their shops on the widest street, which is how it became the main street for the town. Why it wasn't called Main Street,

Lumi couldn't figure out, but it didn't matter to her. She loved it. Sometimes she would imagine what the street looked like all those years ago. Today it was a charming brick-laid street full of beautiful, well-kept businesses and shops. Colorful awnings and blossoming flowers flowing from planters that hung on the lamp posts donned the street from beginning to end. Each window display was carefully planned out and beautifully decorated. If there were a true Main Street, USA, this was it. Yet, what was most charming about the street was the *end* of it. There was a turnabout at the end with a small fountain in the center. But the true beauty was in the meticulously manicured park that overlooked a crystal clear lake that rested beyond the turnabout. It was breathtaking. It was Lumi's favorite spot in the world to sit and think. It seemed to be a place that allowed her to clear her head and feel good about life again.

Her glasses were a different story, however. She most definitely did not feel good about her reading glasses, and she had a great aversion to wearing them. She only had them for a year and it irritated her that she needed them at all. She saw them as a visible symbol of the fact that she was getting older and that irritated her, too. So when she dropped them on the cement floor in her garage and they hit just right, both lenses cracked. She was irritated all over again that she had to pay for new ones. She readily admitted she had a bad attitude, but that didn't make her change how she felt about it. In Lumi's mind, she had the right to be frustrated and unhappy with the entire glasses situation. It seemed that it was simply salt being poured into her wound to make her remember on a day-to-day basis that she was aging.

As Lumi opened the door of *Optimum Optical* toward the end of 7th Avenue she tried to make a vow with herself to be pleasant about the broken lenses. After all it was no one's fault but her own. She wouldn't take it out on the optician, and if there were any other customers there, she wouldn't make them listen to how it happened. She would just be pleasant, hand over the glasses and wait patiently while the new lenses were placed in her frames. Although no one would ever hear it from her, the truth was, she would be glad to have them fixed. Trying to read the newspaper was no fun with all the cracks and readjusting it took in order to read the words. She had worn them, cracked lenses and all, for a week. She was ready to have them fixed.

She hoped she'd be the only one in the shop that morning, but that was not meant to be. She handed over her cracked glasses to optician and found a comfortable place to sit near the window. As soon as she sat down, the outside door opened and an attractive woman who appeared to be in her early thirties entered the shop. Holding her hand was a small blonde-headed boy, around five years old. The child was handsome, even at his young age. *He's going to be a heartbreaker,* Lumi thought with a wistful smile, remembering her own Kyle at that age and how adorable he had been.

The woman led her son to one of the chairs just a few removed from Lumi. Then she sat down beside him. The coffee table was full of magazines and brochures, and there were two coloring books with a can of crayons as well. Both the boy and his mother ignored all those. Instead she reached into her handbag and pulled out an IPod with a small set of headphones. The child placed the headphones on his head and she turned the IPod on and scanned the contents. His face immediately lit up with joy as his favorite songs began playing into his ears. Unselfconsciously he began to sing along in a clear, sweet voice that warmed Lumi's heart.

She leaned over toward the mother. "He has a good ear for music. He sings quite well for his age," she said with a wink and smile.

The woman smiled as well and nodded her head. "I think so. He certainly loves it!"

"What's his favorite?" Lumi asked.

Looking at her son she replied with a big smile, "He loves everything from Beethoven to the Beatles!"

Lumi chuckled, because she loved all of that as well. "Does he play an instrument?"

"Well, he's trying to learn to play the piano, but it's been a bit of a challenge. I know he'll master it in no time!"

Then the woman pulled a small pair of glasses out of her handbag. They were cracked, just as Lumi's were. But there the similarity ended. The little boy's lenses were as thick as the glass in an old coke bottle.

Lumi felt instantly embarrassed that she asked the question about the piano.

The woman was very gracious and gave an assuring smile that she wasn't offended and neither was Henry, her son. She explained that Henry's prognosis, however, was not good. The doctors believed he would be totally blind by the age of ten unless they could find an organ donor with the right eyes.

Stunned and saddened by this news, Lumi reached out her hand to the woman who took it and squeezed it instead of shaking it. "I'm Lumi."

"I'm Deborah," she responded, "and this is Henry, my son."

On an impulse she reached down and held out her hand to Henry. He noticed her gesture and reached for her hand and shook it firmly (for a five-year-old).

He was so adorable, Lumi's heart melted. "Hi, I'm Lumi," she said as she gave his hand a firm but gentle squeeze.

Lumi looked back at Henry's mother. Her beautiful blue eyes were watching Henry intensely with such love and pride. She must have felt Lumi's sadness, however, and said in a positive and reassuring tone, "We have all the confidence in the world that a donor will be found, don't we, Henry?" Henry looked innocently toward his mother and smiled as he nodded his head in an affirmative response and immediately went back to listening to his music.

"It's really okay," Deborah said. "We have nothing to be ungrateful for. We are healthy and happy. We see the situation with Henry's eyes as a gift and a blessing. With diminished sight all of his other senses seem to work at heightened levels. He has talents that others only dream about, and that's because he's had to learn to use his other senses to a degree that most of us never achieve. I think he has such a gift for music because he *hears* it better than any of us."

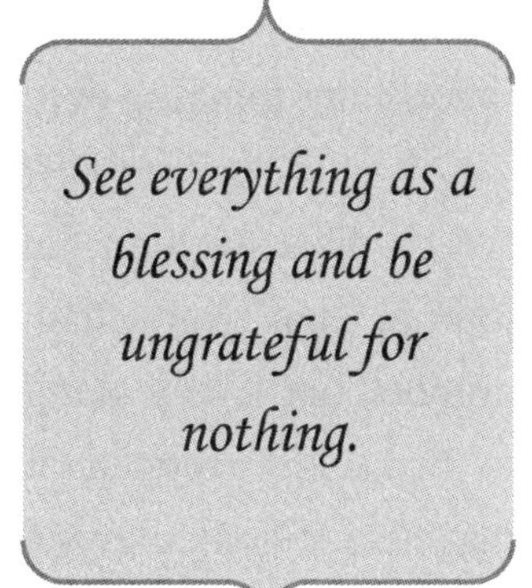

Over the next fifteen minutes while waiting for her repaired glasses, Lumi asked a lot of questions that Deborah answered willingly. Seeing and feeling their gratefulness for something that appeared so unfair and discouraging, Lumi had a hard time believing she had been so upset at breaking her glasses through her own carelessness and also for being so ungrateful for having to wear them in the first place. This amounted to absolutely nothing compared to what many others were challenged with. The gratefulness and acceptance both Henry and his mother exhibited were both humbling and inspiring.

While she was waiting for her glasses, Lumi made two new friends. She and Deborah exchanged phone numbers so that they could meet for lunch the following week as well. Lumi felt a change happening within her just from the twenty minutes she spent in the waiting room of the optical store on 7th Avenue. Never again would she take her eyesight for granted. And never again would she complain about having to wear glasses. She decided to reverse her thinking and be grateful for them.

That evening before going to bed, Lumi located a journal that Kara had given her one Christmas. She grabbed her laptop along with the journal, and carried them to bed. She propped herself up with three pillows then placed her computer strategically on a pillow on her lap and placed the journal beside her on the bed. After an hour of reviewing her e-mails and checking her *Facebook* page she set the computer aside and opened the empty journal that she had yet to write an entry in. There on the first page, written in her best penmanship, was a note from Kara:

To my Mom,
I'm so grateful for you and all that you do.
I Love You,
Kara
Christmas 2008

Lumi leaned back into her pillows and thought for a moment. *I often forget to show gratitude or be grateful for all that I have. I'm going to be more grateful!* At that moment she knew how she would use the journal. She picked up a pen, flipped the page and wrote, *My Journal of*

Gratitude, and signed her name beneath the title. This was for Lumi herself, and she intended to write each day about something for which she was grateful for the rest of her life. Henry had taught her well that day, and it was a lesson she vowed never to forget. There was *so* much to be grateful for! She turned to a new page and wrote these words:

Today I am most thankful for breaking my only pair of reading glasses and the lesson I learned from a five-year-old while having them repaired.

Illumination

Thanksgiving is a day that reminds us to be thankful and grateful; but gratefulness should never be delegated to only one day a year. Practicing gratefulness should be a month to month, day to day, hour to hour and moment to moment event that takes place continuously throughout *every* day of one's entire life. No matter what one's situation, there are always things to be grateful for.

During the *forty-funk*, women often forget all they have to be grateful for. Yet, it's not just women who forget. Unfortunately, many people (male and female) have a *glass-is-half-empty* approach to life where they focus much more on the negatives than the positives. It's not surprising, however, since the media bombards us with one negative situation after another every time we turn on a computer, television, radio or glance at a newspaper.

Yet, even though this happens to us continually, we must remember that every situation contains an opposite. So consider that whenever there is a negative, there always has to be a positive and something to be grateful for. One simply must develop the practice of recognizing, and then focusing on the positive instead of the negative. It's not that we cannot experience the negative, for often it's valid and necessary. The point is simply that you must recognize the negative, and then move out of the emotions and energy it creates. You need to change the energy of the emotion you feel from negativity toward positivity and keep that state of mind.

Consider that whenever there is a negative, there always has to be a positive and something to be grateful for.

Research has shown that those who practice gratefulness actually improve their physical and emotional health. When gratefulness exercises are implemented into a person's life, it has been shown that he or she:

- develops higher levels of positive emotions.
- has more enthusiasm and satisfaction for life.
- has more energy.
- sleeps better.
- is more optimistic.
- has lower levels of stress and depression.
- proves to be more helpful and generous.
- takes better care of himself or herself physically.
- has an improved immune system.

- has higher levels of attentiveness and alertness.
- feels more emotionally balanced.

No matter what a person's circumstances are in life, there are always aspects to be grateful for. Being grateful is a choice. Practicing gratefulness is also a choice. It is critical to develop the habit of being grateful, because without gratitude, a person cannot attract more positive events and people into his or her life. A person attracts what they focus on, thus, the importance of focusing on the positives and good in life rather than the bad and negatives.

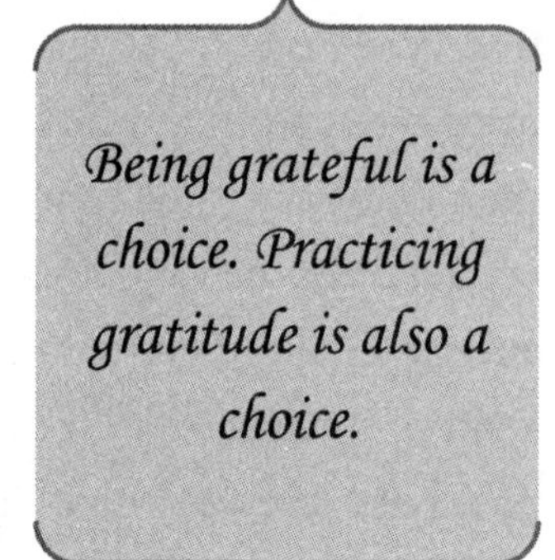

Keeping a *Journal of Gratitude* is a perfect way to remember to practice this gratitude. By keeping a journal and writing in it daily, even if it's only a line or two, keeps you accountable to practicing gratitude. It makes you focus on the good things in your life. It also makes you find good things that happen every day when you don't think there are any. No matter how small, you will find something to write about daily. The more you do this, the more you will find how many wonderful things you actually have going on in your life.

Another way to practice gratitude is before rising in the morning to think about all the things you have to be grateful for and say, *Thank You!* Be grateful for the bed you just slept in, for the hot shower, for the steaming cup of coffee, for the clothes, the technology you have access to, your vehicle, your home and everything else that you have. Be thankful for your health, your ability to walk, talk, hear and see. Be especially thankful for the people in your life… your children, your spouse, your parents, your siblings, your co-workers and your friends. There have to be a few good things about each of these areas and people for which you can be grateful for. Be thankful for the earth in which you live, the sun, the oceans, trees and plants. Often these things are taken for granted, but one must keep in mind that many people don't have all that you have. Be grateful for what you have.

It's also easy to take for granted the special people in your life or to focus on their bad qualities and traits. Maybe you have been rising in the morning only to look to the other side of the bed to find a husband there for whom you no longer have the same feelings as you did years ago. Maybe his mannerisms and habits have become more annoying as the days go on, and you now find them almost intolerable. Maybe your teenage children seem to find pleasure in not listening to you, arguing with you or disobeying the rules of the household. Maybe you don't like their black lipstick, piercings or looking at their

It is difficult to see through or beyond the dark shadows that negatives cast.

pants as they hang half way down their butts and are about to fall off. Maybe your co-workers are lazy, talk on their cell phones all day and complain about their jobs. When you focus on the negative qualities of people, you will find that eventually this is all you will see. Negatives cast such a dark shadow that it makes it difficult to see through it to the good qualities; therefore, it is critical to consciously force yourself to look for and acknowledge the positive qualities these people possess for which you can be grateful.

Maybe your husband has always been faithful, is a good provider and takes out the trash each week. Maybe your child has a beautiful smile, is a good athlete or is polite to your adult friends. Maybe your co-worker always brings you a cup of coffee in the morning when she gets hers. Whatever it may be, no matter how small or insignificant it may appear, be grateful for it. When you start to recognize and appreciate even the tiniest thing in these people or situations, you will find it grows.

When you start to recognize and appreciate even the tiniest thing in people or situations, you will find it grows.

Each day look for new things to be grateful for. Make a game out of it. See if you can find three things each day about each person in your life to be grateful for. Upon waking think of at least five things for which you are grateful. While sitting at stop lights, waiting in lines or even while taking a bathroom break, think of more things for which you are grateful. Then, when you lay your head down on your pillow at night, think about these people once again and recall the things you have discovered about them. As you review, you will find that your gratitude deepens and solidly begins to root and remain firmly planted in your mind. As it does, you will see that what you focus on increases and multiplies.

Though your attitude toward these people in your life may not change all at once, as you start to put this into practice you will find you will feel better toward them and will see more of their good qualities on a regular basis. You will also find that you will tend *not* to focus on the negatives in your life. Instead, you will find more and more positives to be grateful for. As a result, you will become more joyful and want to share that joy with others.

When you live in a state of being thankful and grateful, it changes your life.

When you live in a state of being thankful and grateful, it changes your life.

- Your outlook becomes more positive and appreciative.

- ➢ You begin to see all the good things in life and in people instead of the bad things.
- ➢ You begin to experience all of the physical and emotional benefits of practicing gratitude outlined previously.
- ➢ The joy within you builds, and at the same time you find yourself wanting to give away some of the joy you carry.
- ➢ You find yourself giving your best in every situation—to your job, your family and every life event in which you are involved.
- ➢ You know that you truly feel gratitude when you start becoming a giver to others.
- ➢ You use the words, *thank you,* frequently and genuinely.
- ➢ You are more loving and kind.
- ➢ You look for ways to give appreciation, love, and kindness.
- ➢ You exude such gratefulness that you feel your cup overflows, which is the reason for your desire to share it with others.

Gratitude brings unfathomable blessings to you. Like the ripples in a lake that are touched by a tossed stone, the effects of your gratitude will extend well beyond yourself to others, and then will come back to you in abundance.

Chapter Six: Practicing Kindness

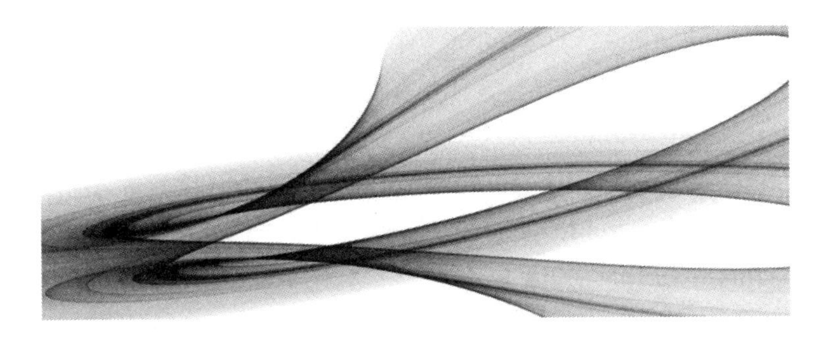

"Always be a little kinder than necessary."
James M. Barrie, Author of the *Lost Boys* (Peter Pan)

Saturday was the day Lumi usually did her shopping and paid her bills. There was no rationale for it, just a habit from the old days when she worked nine to five and did all the errands and household chores on Saturday morning. For some unknown reason she decided to break the habit and just do the only thing that was necessary: shop for groceries. Her friend Laura was coming into town for the night and she wanted to stock up on a few of her favorite items. A trip to the grocery store was a necessity this particular morning.

As she backed the car out of the garage, she noticed her next-door neighbor's son lugging and tugging on a huge box of trash to get it to the curb so it would be picked up by the city workers later in the day. Jimmy was a skinny, eight-year-old, and the box was almost bigger than he was. Lumi giggled at the sight, but decided to put her car in park. She opened the door and stepped across the low flowerbed between the two driveways.

"Wait, Jimmy! I'll help you with that," she called out. Jimmy immediately stopped tugging on the box with a smile of relief on his face.

"Oh, thanks!" he exclaimed as he wiped a few drops of sweat from his brow. "Tommy was supposed to have trash chores this week, but he traded me for picking up the dishes after dinner. He already left for soccer practice so he can't help me."

"It's okay," Lumi responded, "I'll help you."

With the combined muscle power of the two of them, the big box moved quite easily to the curb.

"Thanks Ms. Powers. You're always nice. My mom says you're a kind person. I guess she's right."

Lumi smiled and muttered an embarrassed thank you, went back to her car and continued on her way to the grocery store.

There was a perfectly fine grocery store just two streets over from where Lumi lived, but she loved going to 7th Avenue so much that she chose to do all her shopping there. Not only was the atmosphere of her liking, but that grocery store carried more organic and healthier selections than the one in Lumi's neighborhood. As she drove with all four windows down to enjoy the light breeze and warm sunshine, Lumi kept mulling over the compliment little Jimmy gave her.

Maybe I'm not such a bad person, she thought. She played back the scene in her mind. She remembered noticing that other neighbors were in their yards, moving their own trash to their curbs. They probably would have helped him when they finished. But the truth of the situation was that Lumi was the closest and she just reacted without really thinking about it. She saw a need and reached out to meet it. Anyone would have done the same thing. She dismissed the incident from her mind and in fifteen minutes she was parking in the lot beside Food City.

Before she got out of the car she checked the store's sign for any specials that might interest her. She was surprised to see only one thing on the board: *Change the World Through Kindness.* For a few seconds she just stared at it in surprise at the coincidence of it. *Hmmm,* she thought, *is someone trying to teach me something?* Then she put the entire thing out of her mind as she entered the store and retrieved her shopping list out of her handbag.

> *Change the world through kindness!*

Returning the first cart she chose because it had an annoying habit of pulling to the left, Lumi set out again on her methodical grocery run. She always started on the left of the store so she ended up on the right where the checkout area was when her cart was full. And she always went up and down each aisle looking for bargains and new items featured that week. She especially liked to shop when the demonstrators were handing out samples. She freely admitted she loved to shop for food. *Good thing my metabolism works overtime thanks to Dr. Vida,* she reflected ruefully, *or I'd be two sizes bigger than I am!* She remembered back to how she used to hate to shop because it seemed that when she even looked at food, she gained weight. But now, it seemed that her body was once again working as it had years ago and she only gained weight if she abused her eating, which she was careful not to do.

Lumi turned into the cereal aisle and she saw a toddler running as fast as her chubby legs would go right toward Lumi's cart and away from her mother who was running after her calling, "Annie! Stop! Right this minute!" But Annie had no intention of stopping. Giggling at the top of her voice she ran right into Lumi's outstretched arms as she bent down and scooped her up with a laugh of her own. To her delight, she didn't wiggle to get away but threw her arms around Lumi's neck, giggling the whole time. What could she do but giggle with her?

"Thank you so much!" the mother told Lumi as she reached for her child. "That was nice of you to help me."

Returning the smile a bit absent-mindedly, Lumi muttered something about kindness being an epidemic today and handed the little girl over to her mother, watching as they moved out of sight around the end of the aisle. *Something's going on here and I need a cup of tea to figure it out*, she thought as she headed for the bakery and coffee shop two aisles over.

Once seated with a hot cup of Chi Tea, Lumi pulled out the small notebook she always carried with her. The notebook always gave her something to focus on whenever she sat alone. It had always been a comforting crutch. But lately Lumi was getting better at sitting by herself. Still, the notebook was a nice companion to have when she sat alone.

Obviously the universe was trying to get through to her today with a message of kindness. She wrote *kindness* at the top of a blank page and then waited for some insights. She didn't have to wait long. The thoughts just kept flowing into her mind and she scribbled as fast as she could so she didn't lose them. After a few minutes of furious concentration, she put the pen down and looked at what she wrote.

What is kindness?
A desire to do good things to help people with no thought of getting anything in return.

Perform random acts of kindness daily.
Think kind thoughts.
Give appreciation and compliments to everyone who moves in and out of your day.

How can I be kind
to my neighbors?

Pay attention to what's going on around me and assist where I can.

to strangers?

Do what I can to help as opportunities arise.

to myself?

Stop beating myself up when I mess up.

Improve on things within my power to change for the better, while accepting those things that are out of my control to change.

Make kindness your state of being through your thoughts, words and actions!

Make kindness my state of being through my thoughts, words and actions.

Lumi couldn't believe she'd written all that, but she must have because her cup of tea was empty. *That's awesome,* she thought in amazement. *Now I'd better hustle and finish my shopping because I have to pick Laura up at the airport this afternoon. I'm always happy to catch up with an old friend from college. We'll have a good time on her visit, even though it's only for 24 hours. Too bad she has to leave right away. I'm glad I'm not the one flying cross-country, but it was nice of her to plan a stopover here with me.*

Lumi completed her shopping and headed home. All the way she thought about kindness and how she could be more aware of opportunities to practice it every day. She finally decided that since the universe was doing such a good job teaching her so far, she should just relax and trust that when she was supposed to do something kind, it would be clear to her what she should do. Maybe practicing kindness would become second nature to her. She hoped so because she decided she enjoyed being grateful and spreading kindness!

Mid-afternoon Lumi left for the airport to meet Laura. She arrived half an hour early, parked and walked to the correct terminal. She went to the arrival monitor right away and looked for her flight number. It was on time. And so was she. The airport was very busy this afternoon, and Lumi was glad she had left plenty of time to get there and park the car.

Then she noticed a petite elderly lady—probably no more than five feet tall and ninety pounds soaking wet. She was dressed completely in black, including a black kerchief, double-knotted under her chin, covering her white hair. She was standing about ten feet away staring up at all the screens and then down at the airline ticket she clutched in her hand. Up and down, up and down. It was abundantly apparent the woman was confused and uncertain what to do. Thinking someone in the crowd of people rushing past her in all directions would stop and assist the little woman in black, Lumi waited to see what would happen. No one stopped. Lost in their own little worlds, no one offered to help her or even notice her. One word popped into Lumi's mind: *kindness*. She moved a step closer and said, "Do you need a little help?"

The woman's response said it all. She smiled and her face crinkled up and she began explaining her situation to Lumi, who nodded and smiled continuously to reassure the woman. There was only one problem. She wasn't speaking English.

Lumi searched for a way to communicate with the woman. She pointed at the ticket and the woman handed it to her with a trusting smile. Lumi got the flight number off the ticket, checked the monitor and discovered there was enough time to walk the woman to the right gate where, hopefully, someone would speak her language. But how to get her to go with her was the question. How could she let the confused and frightened woman know she would get her where she had to go? And then it occurred to her.

The woman was wearing an ornate silver crucifix around her neck. It was her only piece of jewelry other than a plain gold wedding band. Hoping that the woman would understand, Lumi pointed at the woman's crucifix and smiled broadly from her heart. The woman nodded and a beautiful smile lit up her face all the way to her eyes. Lumi smiled back, gave the woman back her ticket and motioned for her to come with her. Then the two of them headed toward the correct gate several hundred feet away.

It took about ten minutes to get there and Lumi began to wonder if she'd make it to Laura's gate before her friend emerged from the plane. Well, if she didn't, Laura would have sense enough to wait for her. Her new friend needed her right now and that was her first priority. When they arrived at the gate, Lumi walked the woman right up to the attendant handling the boarding. A few words explained the situation and the attendant smiled at the little woman and held her hand out for the ticket. Although she looked at Lumi for confirmation that it was okay to hand the ticket over, one nod and a smile was all she needed.

By then it was time for Lumi to dash back to meet Laura. She wondered how to say goodbye to the little lady she had befriended. She looked into the woman's eyes, smiled and gave her a gentle hug which the woman warmly returned. The woman in black then began speaking rapidly in her own language. Lumi didn't understand a word of it, but she had a good idea what was being said. Lumi pointed to her watch, waved goodbye and took off at an easy run toward the gate where Laura was going to appear at any moment.

Just as she arrived at the gate, Laura emerged from the jet way. They hugged and Laura asked why she was out of breath. Lumi grinned and replied, "The kindness bug showed up, and it took me a little out of my way!"

They walked toward baggage claim, and as they got on the escalator to ride down to the next level Lumi noticed a large poster on the wall with a saying that struck a chord with her.

It read…

> "Thousands of candles can be lighted from a single candle, and the life of the candle will not be shortened. Happiness never decreases by being shared."
> Buddha

Hmmm, she thought, *all I've been doing for the past few years is feeling sorry for myself. I was having my own pity-party; and as a result, I think I shut myself off from the world and didn't notice what was going on around me. I didn't notice other people, and I didn't notice opportunities for kindness.*

But when I do kind things for others, I feel good, and it seems to open me up to the world. Or.... is it that I'm opening up to the world, and as a result feel better about myself so I perform acts of kindness? Either way, she thought, *it's a good thing.*

She glanced at the poster one more time as she exited the escalator. Instead of reading it as it was, she translated it to: *Thousands of acts of kindness can be performed by one individual, and the life of that individual will not be diminished. Kindness never decreases one's blessings by being shared. It increases them.*

Illumination

Most people remember Aesop's famous fable about the *Lion and the Mouse.* In the fable, the lion was awakened by a mouse running across him. The lion reaches out his huge paw and opens his large jaws to eat him. The mouse begs his forgiveness and promises that if the lion were to let him go, he would someday return the favor and save his life. The lion chuckles to think a mouse could possibly return such a favor, but through an act of kindness, he lets the mouse go. Later, the lion is captured by hunters and bound by ropes. He roars loudly in the hopes that someone may help him, and the mouse hears the roars and comes to his rescue. The mouse gnaws and gnaws at the ropes until the lion is free and his life is saved. The moral of the story is: No act of kindness, no matter how small, is ever wasted. [Aesop, Greek Slave and fable author (620 BC – 560 BC)] (3).

A random act of kindness is always worthwhile whether toward others, the universe or yourself. Though unlike Aesop's fable, kindness does not necessarily come back from the same person to whom you were kind or in the same form, but it *will* come back to you. Whenever you emit positive energy into the universe (as in the form of kindness), it can't help but come back to you in a positive manner. Even scientifically, research has shown that acts of kindness benefit the giver both psychologically and physically. Knowing you have done something kind creates a sense of connectedness to that individual and to the universe. In the publication, *The Healing Power of Doing Good*, studies showed physical responses such as a greater sense of relaxation, less stress, calmness, decreased blood pressure and increased energy when an act of kindness is performed (4).

Being a kind person can change your life, your heart and the world. According to *The Secret*, by Rhonda Byrne, "Every good thought you think, every good word you speak, every good emotion you feel, and every act of kindness you perform, is lifting the frequency of your being to new heights. And as you begin to raise your frequency, a new life and a new world will reveal themselves to you. You will emit positive forces of energy. You will lift yourself, and as you lift yourself, you lift the entire world" (5). Note that it doesn't say that it will *only* lift others. *You* will be lifted by it as well. Kindness is not a one-way street. It benefits many.

Being a kind person can change your life, your heart and the world!

Yet most importantly, be kind to yourself. Most women were raised as nurturers and givers. Because of this, they often put their own needs on the back burner. It's just as important to be as kind to yourself as you are to others. Some examples of practicing kindness toward yourself may be to:

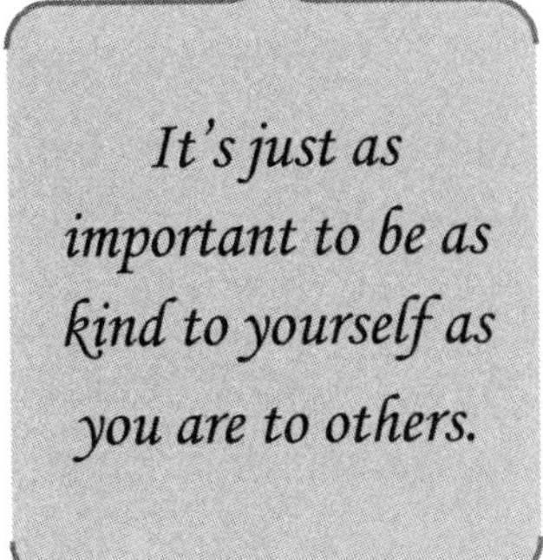

- Remember to speak kindly toward yourself. Focus on your wonderful qualities, and speak to yourself as if you were a friend.
- Take time for yourself. Pamper yourself now and then with a massage, pedicure or facial. Go to a movie or dinner with friends. Go for a walk, or do whatever it is that may give you some joy.
- Relax. Who says you can't put your pajamas on at six P.M. and lie on the couch and watch a movie?
- Forgive yourself for anything that you haven't.
- Smile. A smile always comes back to you.
- Give yourself a day off from cooking and cleaning.

- Get creative and find ways to be kind to yourself.

Kindness is simply acting kind toward someone or something with no expectation of anything in return. It's done simply out of the goodness of your heart. Ask yourself one simple question: "Am I being kind?" It can change your life. If you approach each day being cognitive of whether or not you are acting in a kind manner and then take actions that are kind, you will find that you not only make someone else's day a little brighter, but that brightness will be reflected back to you. Never underestimate the power of a kind word, a smile, an honest compliment, a warm greeting, or assisting anyone in need no matter how small that act may be.

Ask yourself one simple question: "Am I being kind?" It can change your life.

There are many opportunities daily to be kind. Don't let them pass you by. Gandhi believed, "To give pleasure to a single heart by a single act of kindness is better than a thousand heads bowing in prayer." Let kindness be a way of life and extend some form of kindness toward someone every single day for a period of two weeks. The more you practice kindness, the sooner you will find that it becomes second nature and a habit. The result: You make a difference in others' lives, and you change your world to a kinder one.

Chapter Seven: Relationships

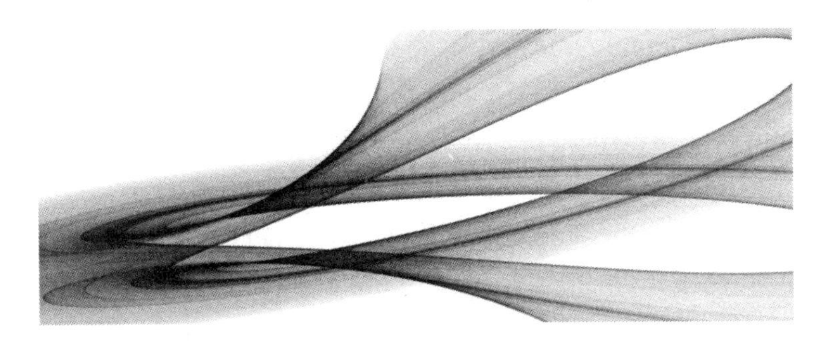

"If you realized how powerful your thoughts are, you would never think a negative thought."
Peace Pilgrim

By eight A.M. Tuesday morning, Lumi was just entering her usual parking spot just around the corner of 7th Avenue. She was ninety minutes early for her appointment with Dr. Vida and was excited about seeing her. This was her monthly check-in, and she could hardly wait to share all the things that happened to her since her last visit.

Since she hadn't eaten breakfast yet, she planned to go to *Chuck's Corner Store* and read the morning paper and enjoy a cup of coffee. Maybe she'd splurge and have a mocha latte. *Chuck's* had sidewalk tables that were popular with the locals, and it also carried all the local daily newspapers, including some national ones. It sounded relaxing.

She entered *Chuck's* to pick up the paper and the latte. Inside the shop, the flat-screen TV above the counter was spouting negative news: Shootings in California, the highest unemployment rate in twenty years, thousands of homes in foreclosure.... She didn't want to hear any of it right now. The people in the shop were glued to the screen, hanging onto every detail of the disasters that were bombarding the country. It reminded her of September 11th when no one could even think of anything else, much less move away from the television and radio. If she didn't get out of there right now, she'd end up falling into the same addictive behavior, entranced by the seductive, negative news!

With the latte and a copy of *The Daily Sun* under her arm, she settled down at a table for two under a shade umbrella. She scanned everything on the front page of the paper and found nothing she felt like reading. War, famine, disasters, and the economy—she just wasn't up to all that this morning. She was feeling great and didn't want to lose her positive outlook and energy by filling her mind with depressing and negative stuff. *Seems as if all the news is bad,* she thought. *Why can't there be some good news for a change? Maybe things are better on the local front.* She turned to the back page of the community section (also the very last page of the paper), and a headline caught her eye: *Mrs. Bennett Comes Clean.* She knew that woman! What had Denise done now?

As it turned out Denise Bennett hadn't done anything, at least nothing unusual for her. Fed up with the growing mountains of trash at the local recycling facility, two years ago she started an environmentally friendly company that supplied green products to the hospitality industry. She shopped for the products, purchased them in bulk at a discount, and resold them to the motels, hotels, restaurants and other hospitality-related businesses. To her surprise, the business grossed over ten million dollars last year, which was why she was featured in today's *Daily Sun.*

I like that, Lumi thought. *Good for Denise. I should give her a call and meet her for lunch. She's always so fun. It would be good for me.*

Lumi flipped backward through the rest of the paper looking for something else uplifting to read. She didn't find anything on the first flip-through, so she flipped through again, this time from front to back. Nothing. Zip. Plenty of news, though. All negative. Even the cartoons emphasized the negative. Lumi had enough negatives in her life. What she wanted now was to surround herself with positive things. But then she realized something.

Lumi had enough negatives in her life. What she wanted now was to surround herself with positive things.

Just a few months ago I couldn't seem to get out of my own way. Nothing was going right in my life and I dreaded getting out of bed each morning. I expected things to go wrong, and they did. I focused on the negatives in the world. I had no hope, no excitement and no inner happiness or joy. That wasn't a good time in my life. Then I met Dr. Vida and learned how to take better care of myself. My life is more positive and interesting, and I bounce out of bed looking forward to the day. I did what they call a one-eighty. Why can't the newspapers and the rest of the media do the same thing? I know bad things happen and we do need to be kept informed, but how about a little more balance in the news coverage?

She recalled something author, Wayne Dyer, had written, "The state of your life is nothing more than a reflection of your state of mind." *Hmmm*, she thought, *the media contributes to this big time!*

> *"The state of your life is nothing more than a reflection of your state of mind."*
> *Wayne Dyer*

Still pondering the state of the media, Lumi walked to the bakery counter and bought a low-fat blueberry muffin to go with the last of her latte. She glanced up at the television once again only to see and hear a newscaster recite the details of a horrific murder with as much enthusiasm as if she had just won the lottery. As the clerk handed Lumi the muffin, he noticed the alarmed look on her face and questioned her, “Is everything okay?”

Lumi looked back and saw the kind, thin, familiar face of the owner. Chuck was an icon in the town. He had owned the corner store for years, and although he was in his eighties, he never missed a day of working the counter.

“Oh, I was just noticing that all the news on TV is so negative. How can you stand to have it on all day long?” She asked.

“You know,” he paused, as he wiped down the counter in front of her, “watching it is a choice. I give my customers what they want, but I don’t *choose* to watch it.” He leaned into the counter a bit and propped his boney elbows in front of her and whispered, “It will bring you down you know. You have to be careful.”

Lumi smiled and nodded her head in agreement.

“I know,” she whispered back. She picked up her muffin, smiled once again at Chuck and sat down again at her table. She thought back over her own history.

All her life she had been a positive person, seeing the glass half-full and not half-empty. She was always the one to point out the bright side of things to everyone else. She was the one who always was able to find a positive in every situation, no matter how negative it appeared to be. When any of her friends had been down or faced a difficult situation, it was Lumi to whom they went to for help. She always cheered them up. She had been everyone else’s champion, cheering them on, encouraging them to focus on the positive things they still had instead of the things they lost.

Yet trouble is not discriminatory; it touches everyone at one time or another. There had been a time in Lumi's past when it seemed that, like the newspaper, her life was filled with negativity and difficulty. The people she was closest to back then—friends, the man she loved, her coworkers—all had problems of their own, and they shared them freely with her because she was such a good listener. None of them offered to listen to Lumi's own struggles, however, so she internalized them and never had the opportunity to talk them out. Her husband's business was a constant source of stress for both of them, her mother was dying of cancer, and she had the wonderful, but demanding, twins who were wearing her out physically. She also had a perfectionist mentality that made her feel as though she was never good enough. She always felt she came up short emotionally and physically. It was difficult to always have to pretend to be so up-beat and positive for everyone when she felt so tired, stressed and alone inside. To top it all off came her most difficult days when she was faced with a divorce.

That was when Denise, her husband and children moved into the house next door. Determined to be a good neighbor in spite of her sadness and low energy, Lumi took out a box of Bisquick to make a batch of biscuits and pulled an unopened jar of strawberry jam off the pantry shelf to welcome her new neighbors. That sacrificial act had paid great dividends in the nearly twelve-year friendship she and Denise shared.

Her twins had been a constant source of blessing to her as well. It was so wonderful to see them stepping out on their own as young adults. In eighteen months they would both have their undergraduate degrees, Kara in English and Kyle in Marketing. She was so proud of them! She had much for which to give thanks. And now that her physical and emotional health was returning under Dr. Vida's guidance and care, life was good once again.

There's only one area of my life now that still concerns me a bit, Lumi mused. *It's my thoughts. I can get so down sometimes! Just hearing all that negative news makes me feel discouraged and I don't want to get that way again. Garbage in, garbage out,* she remembered. *I need to filter what I allow to enter my mind. I need to focus on positive things and what makes me feel good about life. No more negative input!* To seal the promise she'd just made to herself, she threw the newspaper into the trash bin on her way to Dr. Vida's office.

> *Filter what you allow to enter your mind. Focus on positive things and what makes you feel good about life. No more negative input!*

Things went well at her doctor's appointment. One thing surprised her though. Dr. Vida reminded her that she needed to take care of herself and not worry so much about meeting other people's needs. As she pointed out to Lumi, if she didn't take care of herself, who would? It was okay to be optimistic and encouraging to others, but not at her own expense. It was time to take care of Lumi for a change.

"Lumi," she said, "you have a caregiver mentality. It's in your personality to give, give and give. You are a great encourager and builder-upper to everyone except yourself. You make people feel good about themselves, which attracts them to you. I enjoy you as a person and as a patient and I see the wonderful qualities you possess. But I've also noticed that you are very hard on yourself. You really need to change that. *You're* the only one who thinks you're not doing a great job at being a successful human being. Don't you know the rest of us think you're awesome?"

And then Dr. Vida really surprised her by handing her a gift. She even wrapped it in gift paper and added a beautiful bow. Lumi was speechless. She could hardly undo the bow and unwrap the gift. When she finally had it unwrapped, she found a silver dove ornament with an inscription on it: *Love yourself first, and everything else falls into place.* Lumi couldn't speak. She was so touched. She looked up at the doctor who had become her friend, but she couldn't speak. She finally whispered, "Thank you. From the bottom of my little heart."

Dr. Vida smiled, shook her head and said, “Lumi, Lumi. There’s *nothing* little about your heart.”

At that Lumi forced a big smile to prevent herself from crying, but tears still ran down her cheeks in gratitude. Even Dr. Vida brushed back a few tears—tears of joy for the wonderful woman who was finally realizing her own worth.

Later that afternoon after Lumi returned home, she called Denise. She answered on the second ring.

“Denise?”

“That would be me!” a cheerful voice answered.

“This is Lumi.”

“Hi Lumi. It’s so good to hear from you! How are you and what are you doing these days?”

“I’m doing well, thanks. I’m calling to congratulate you on the great article in the paper this morning. Well done!”

“Thank you. No one was more surprised than I was to get an article in the paper. It’s amazing how a good idea can multiply, isn’t it?”

“Yours certainly did! I’m impressed! I was wondering if you’d be interested in having lunch sometime soon. We could catch up on the news, and I’d love to see you again. We always had such great laughs together, didn’t we?”

“We did! I’d like that. I just had my calendar in my hand when you called. Let’s see. Would the day after tomorrow work for you?”

"Absolutely. Let's meet at *Marfrisco's* for lunch. Would that be okay? About noon?"

"Perfect! I'll be there. I'm so glad you called, Lumi. You popped into my mind just last week and I thought I should call you; and here you are calling me! Isn't that amazing?"

"I don't believe in coincidences, Denise. Our lunch date was meant to be. I'm looking forward to it. See you then!"

After they both said good-bye and hung up, Lumi still sat at her kitchen table with a big smile on her face thinking how good it was to have positive, uplifting friends. Sure, everyone goes through difficult times, but a positive attitude carries you throughout the day. Lumi thought, *from now on I just want to surround myself with positive people and positive news. I've had enough down time lately to last me the rest of my life!*

A positive attitude carries you throughout the day. From now on I just want to surround myself with positive people and positive news.

Illumination

There are several types of relationships in which we engage throughout our lives such as those we are born into with our parents, siblings and relatives. There are those we choose with our friends, spouse, work-out buddies and acquaintances. Some relationships are forced upon us such as with co-workers or neighbors.

We can also choose to engage in relationships that form through different forms of media. We can develop pseudo-relationships with the people in reality television shows, with the broadcasters of the nightly news, with columnists in the newspaper and even with characters in movies. We look forward to seeing them weekly, hearing what they have to say, relating to them and even loving or hating them. As an example, many people have formed relationships with people on the reality TV shows *Survivor, American Idol, The Real World, The Bachelor, Amazing Race* and so many others. They talk about each episode relating their likes and dislikes toward every person in the show. They cheer on some while hope for the demise of others. These shows also show the varying degrees of relationships and how others can be affected by each person in their lives.

Some relationships can prove positive and uplifting, while others are detrimental and negative. It's the same in the *real* world. Some of our relationships can be life-giving, while others can be energy-draining and difficult.

Some relationships can prove positive and uplifting, while others are detrimental and negative.

Choosing relationships can be critical to your mental state of being. Surrounding yourself with motivational, positive people who have your best interests at heart is a wise decision. There will be no drama, no competition, and no back stabbing. When you choose healthy relationships, you will find that they are extremely easy most of the time.

On the same note, you will instinctively know when you are *not* involved in good relationships. You may find them exhausting, difficult, negative, and that they bring you down or cause you stress. The media can be a negative relationship that has a way of doing this. When a person is bombarded with negative news, all cells in the body respond to this negativity; and when a person is exposed to negativity that causes stress, the body releases adrenaline to fight it. When a person is exposed to negativity and stress over and over, the body develops a resistance and adapts to the situation by secreting hormones that increase blood pressure and blood sugars. A prolonged overuse of this resistance and adaption can lead to mental fatigue, irritability, lethargy, anxiety and disease in the body. The hormone, Cortisol, is high during these periods and can interfere with Serotonin levels which can increase depression, cause weight gain, insomnia and depress the immune system.

Yet the body is an amazing vehicle and can fight against these negative influences and effects simply by engaging in positive influences. Positive influences have proven to help restore feelings of hope and self-esteem and increase the immune system. Surrounding yourself with positive people, reading only uplifting news, watching only educational or optimistic television programming can begin to make you feel better about every aspect of your life. Removing yourself from situations of negativity can be one of the best things you have ever done for yourself. Turn off the negativity, exploitation and humiliation that some television shows thrive on. Don't read newspapers or magazines that do the same. Know what is going on in the world, but don't immerse yourself in the sensationalism and doom and gloom that is projected by every newscaster.

Positive influences have proven to help restore feelings of hope and self-esteem and increase the immune system.

Remove yourself from relationships that cause you harm or mental distress.

Keep in mind that no one can force their negativity upon you. Only *you* can allow negativity to enter your life by dropping to the level of frequency in which negativity thrives. Positive feelings raise your energy to a higher level (or higher frequency). Negative feelings cannot rise to that level; however, positive feelings *can* fall to a lower level where negativity thrives if you allow it to do so. An easy way to determine what frequency you are on is this: When you feel joy, you are most likely on a higher frequency. When you feel angst, you are most likely on a lower level of frequency. So set your thoughts and feelings on a higher, more positive level of energy and frequency. As a result it becomes almost impossible for negativity to affect you. Negativity cannot rise to that level, and it will be unable to penetrate your thoughts and unable to create adverse affects in your life.

Positive feelings raise your energy to a higher level (or higher frequency).

Everyone emits a frequency, and typically everyone in your life is on a similar frequency as you.

Everyone emits a level of energy or frequency. To understand this a little better, think about how in-tune animals are to frequencies. For example, a horse or dog will immediately know if you are scared. They will feel that vibration. Many of us have also experienced a pet that somehow knows we are sad or upset about something. As I mentioned, everyone emits a frequency, and typically everyone in your life is on a *similar* frequency as you. Therefore, if everyone in your life is negative, take a good, hard look in the mirror. On the same note, the more you step away from negativity and move toward positivity, the more you will see amazing things happen in your life. You will begin to attract those with a more positive frequency. You will find that you no longer attract negative people and negative events into your life. The more you engage in only positive relationships, positive situations and positive thinking, the more you will find that you attract more of the same.

One of most important relationships you will have is with your spouse or partner. You probably have experienced or heard others say, "I somehow keep attracting the same kind of person. I always attract a guy who is addicted to drugs or alcohol. Why do I always get into abusive relationships? Every man I've been with has cheated on me."

Why do people seem to repeat the same types of relationships? One answer may be that it's karma to work out. It could also be that you *aren't* destined to repeat unhappy and difficult relationships over and over again. Maybe you are simply focusing on what you *don't* want instead of what you *do* want! *You get what you focus on*!

People are so worried about repeating a bad relationship that they focus on *not* wanting to get involved with a person that would repeat such a relationship or behavior; and time and time again, that is exactly what they attract. It's time to change your thinking from what you *don't* want to what you *do* want!

It's time to change your thinking from what you don't want to what you do want!

Write a list of every quality that a person *must* have in order to *deserve* to be in a relationship with you! List ONLY the positive, good qualities that you want in a person. List no less than twenty-five qualities. Then post the list on your bathroom mirror and read it daily. Visualize only a person with these qualities coming into your life. Eventually this is what you will get. You will be amazed with the results, and I guarantee you will be telling all of your single friends to give it a try.

This doesn't *just* work when you are looking for a mate. This works for your children, current partner, and others. Write lists of all the positive qualities you see and *want* to see in your children, your partner and others who are important in your life. Though you can't directly change these people, you can focus on only those traits you want to see when you interact with them. This will create a more positive relationship with each of them when you focus on appreciating and remembering only their wonderful qualities.

And finally, do this for yourself. Write a list of all the qualities you want to possess. Describe exactly how you see yourself as the person you aspire to be. Never write anything negative, only positive things. Read it daily and remind yourself how *fabulous* you really are! Remember, the most important relationship you have is with yourself.

Chapter 8:
Visualization and Faith

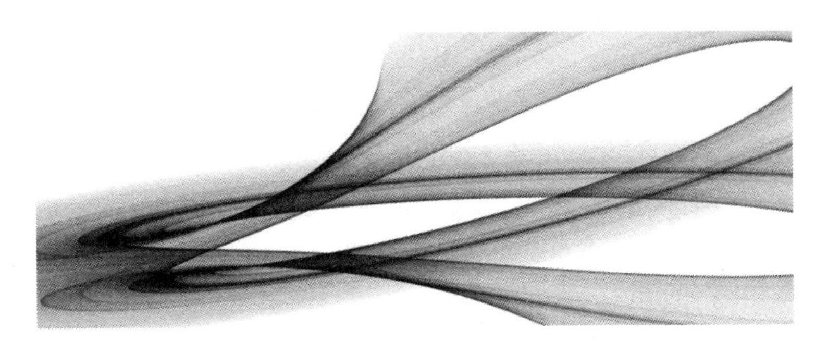

"Take the first step in faith. You don't have to see the whole staircase—just the first step."
Dr. Martin Luther King Jr.

After a wonderful lunch at *Marfrisco's*, Denise and Lumi hugged each other goodbye. They had spent the past two hours sharing all the positive things going on in each of their lives. *How nice not to have focused on negative things for a change. I feel empowered and energized by all the positive things we talked about today. I need to make it a point to spend more time with her,* she thought as her friend walked away.

Lumi wasn't ready to go home. She was feeling so energized and positive that she wanted to enjoy more of the day on 7th Avenue, so she decided to do a little window shopping. Everything she looked at she thought, *How beautiful!* The baskets that hung from the lamp posts were overflowing with flowers. *How beautiful*! The displays in the windows were beautiful! The baby in the carriage that passed her was beautiful. She even glanced and caught her reflection in the window once and saw herself with a big, bright smile and thought, *Wow, even I'm beautiful today!* It was a wonderful day, and Lumi felt glorious! That was the only word she could think of to describe it.

Her thoughts were interrupted by the sliding of several minivan doors opening to fifteen young boys in baseball uniforms leaping from their seats onto the sidewalk. Their cleats clicked-clacked on the pavement as they ran to the ice cream shop just ahead of Lumi. They were all jumping up and down with happy smiles shouting, "We won. We won!" The tinkling of the bell on the ice cream shop's door was inviting, and Lumi decided to follow the band of excitement and energy inside. She couldn't help but smile, too, as she looked at all the smiling faces of the boys.

The large handbag that Lumi was carrying at her side was bumped.

"Excuse me, ma'am," she heard.

Lumi looked down to see a little boy with dark brown hair and deep, dark brown eyes. He had a beautiful grin across his face.

"It's okay," responded Lumi. "So what was the score?" She asked, obviously assuming the boys had won.

With the same big smile and confidence he responded, "Zero to zero so far!"

Puzzled, Lumi asked, "What do you mean?"

"We haven't played the game yet!" he chuckled. "Coach always takes us out for ice cream after practice the day *before* the game to celebrate winning the next day. Coach makes us celebrate playing our best *before* playing our game. I'm going to hit three homers tomorrow! And my friend Josh is going to pitch a no-hitter!"

Lumi looked up toward the counter and saw an older, very fit man wearing a baseball hat and shirt that had the word COACH printed on the back. He had as big a smile as the boys did as he helped them place their ice cream orders. She then looked back down at this little boy.

"Your coach is a very smart man."

"He sure is, ma'am. He helped us all make winner's boards, and you know what? It works! We made a team winner's board with all of our pictures with thumbs up and stuff playing baseball. On mine I have a picture of the new glove I want. I had a picture of a bat and Red Sox baseball jersey that I wanted, too, and you know what? I got it! I got it for my birthday! I just turned eight!"

"Well, Happy Birthday," Lumi said with kindness in her voice. "I hope you have a great game tomorrow."

"We will. We always do," he said with such confidence, "We always have fun no matter what!"

That's what it's about, Lumi thought as her eyes followed him to the line at the counter. These boys see what they want, but mostly, they see themselves having a great time. She decided to sit down at one of the smaller tables and enjoy the spectacle.

Coach had glanced over at Lumi as she was speaking to his player, and once orders were placed and payment had been made, he worked his way over to her.

"Don't say it," he chuckled as he shook his head with a grin. "You may think I'm crazy, but there's something to it—really! Maybe it's just that it gets them really excited and in a positive frame of mind. Maybe it's the encouragement from each other they get. Maybe it's because they really see themselves as winners, but these boys are having a great time and achieving a lot of their goals."

"I actually love that you do this," Lumi responded, "but I have a question. What happens if they lose?"

The coach's smile grew bigger. "It's not about actually winning. It's about doing the best you can. I teach the boys that they are *always* winners if they give it their best effort. They know I don't really care about the score in the end. I just want them to feel good about themselves, their efforts and their teammates. Winning is being a good sport when you win *and* when you don't win. It's about being a good teammate and having a good time."

"Well, I think what you are teaching them is beautiful!" Lumi said as she realized there was that word again. Everything today was beautiful! She giggled to herself, "Good luck, Coach!"

Still with big smiles and excitement, Lumi watched as each child finished his ice cream and then piled back into the vans in which they had come. She rose and stepped to the counter and ordered a child-size vanilla ice cream cone with rainbow sprinkles on it.

That evening Lumi dug into her craft drawer and pulled out colored pencils, markers, glue and paper. She also found a big piece of poster board that had been left over from a school project that her kids had worked on, as well as several old magazines. She clipped and cut pictures out, including some motivational words that resonated with her. Then she went to work gluing them in no particular order all over the board. She had a picture of a new convertible she wanted, the words SMILE and ABUNDANCE, and a picture of Central Park in New York. Knowing what was missing, she started rummaging in a drawer looking for pictures. There she found a photo of herself at her perfect weight, as well as a photo of her with Kyle and Kara on vacation, all smiling and happy. She pasted these photos in a prominent place on the board. This board had just become her vision board—a board that would remind her of all the things she wanted in her life.

Stepping back and looking at it, Lumi felt good. *I wonder*, she thought, and then quickly grabbed a piece of paper and started writing and drawing on it. Getting up from the table, she practically ran into her office and grabbed a hard-cover book off the bookshelf and quickly tore off its paper cover. She ran back to the table and carefully folded the paper she had been drawing on over the book. She made four folds so that it fit perfectly over the book exactly as the original cover had fit and laid it back on the table. In front of her was a book that now symbolized her novel, yet to be written, but soon to be finished. It even said, *NY Times Best Seller* on it! At that moment she began to *see* her book as finished and published.

With her new vision tools in her hand she walked into her office and placed the book on a small picture stand on her desk to inspire her as she wrote. She then carried her new vision board into her bedroom so that she would be able to look at it before falling asleep each night.

Once tucked into bed that evening she thought about her day, the baseball players, the coach and her own vision board and book. *There's something else that's missing*, she thought. A bit embarrassed by her desire, but determined not to be, she opened her bedroom night-stand's top drawer and pulled out a notebook. On the top of the page she wrote, QUALITIES A MAN MUST HAVE IN ORDER TO DESERVE ME. Under this heading she began to list all of the characteristics she wished for in a partner. When finished with her list of twenty-five qualities, she tore the page out of the notebook, got out of bed and found some tape, and then taped the list to her bathroom mirror. *There*, she thought, *now I'm finished.*

Illumination

Winston Churchill once said, "You create your own universe as you go along." These words are encouraging in that your life isn't necessarily pre-destined. It allows for the possibility that you actually are in charge of creating your life. These words empower you to believe that you have some control over your future—control you probably long for but aren't certain you actually have at this stage of your life.

> *"You create your own universe as you go along."*
> *Winston Churchill*

According to the *Webster Dictionary* faith is defined as *"belief and trust in and loyalty to God; belief in the traditional doctrines of a religion; firm belief in something for which there is no logical proof or material evidence; complete trust; something that is believed especially with strong conviction"* (7). When you read this definition, it basically says that you have to believe in something that you can't see, hear, touch or feel. If something has no logical proof or material evidence, then how are you expected to see it and believe it? The logical answer obviously is *faith*, but the concept of believing in something when there is no visual confirmation feels like something is missing.

Yet there is a difference between *blind* faith and *visualized* faith. Blind faith, with no visual picture of the life you want to live or the things you want to have in your life, would not get you the results you want. You actually *need* visual confirmation! You actually have to have enough *faith* to *see it* in order to *believe it!*

In 1937 Napoleon Hill wrote in *Think and Grow Rich*, "Whatever the mind of man can conceive, and believe, it can achieve." Andrew Carnegie said basically the same thing stating, "Anything the mind of man can see, and believe, he can achieve." Some of the most brilliant and most successful human beings on this earth believed in a similar philosophy. They all kept coming back to the fact that you have to *see* it (visualize it) in order to achieve it.

> *"Whatever the mind of man can conceive, and believe, it can achieve."*
> *Napoleon Hill*

The problem, however, is that many only *see* their *current* circumstances, which is often *not* what they want in their lives. When people think about what they currently have, that's all they continue to get. You *achieve* what you *see.* Therefore, it's critical to eliminate those thoughts from your mind and create new pictures and new visions based on what you would *like* to have in your life. This is the visualized piece. Then you have to add faith—faith that your visualizations will be achieved.

Sidney Madwed stated, "Our subconscious minds have no sense of humor, play no jokes and cannot tell the difference between our reality and an imagined thought or image. What we continually think about eventually will manifest in our lives."

This is a time of great reflection. This is your opportunity to change your future by seeing it as you wish it, not how it currently is. You must always keep in mind that, "You are today where your thoughts have brought you; you will be tomorrow where your thoughts take you." James Allen.

This is your opportunity to change your future by seeing it as you wish it, not how it currently is.

Where do you want to be tomorrow? Whom do you want in your life? What do you want to be doing? How do you see your life?

Philosopher and author, Jim Rohn, stated, "I found that when you start thinking and saying what you really want, your mind automatically shifts and pulls you in that direction. And sometimes it can be that simple." Start thinking about what you want. Start speaking about what you want. There is no dream too big. You can have the life you want and be the person you want if you create a clear vision of what that looks like. The key is to believe in your visualized visions. Then *believe* that you will *receive* whatever it is that you want. Whatever you see and live on the inside first will eventually manifest on the outside. Your entire life begins on the inside first.

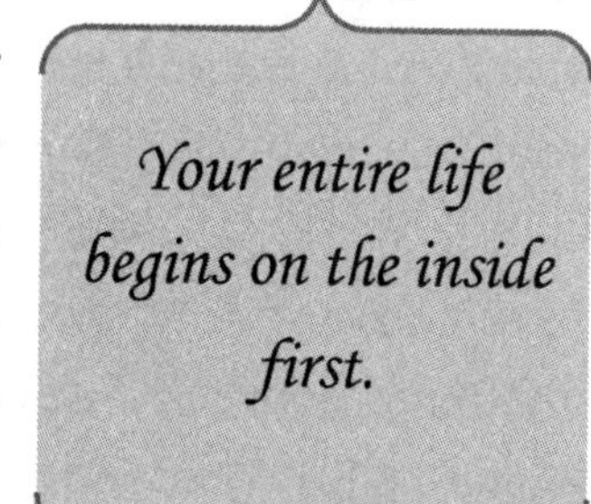

There are several tools to help you do this. Start with a list. Write out all the things you would like in your life. Write a description of your perfect life and how you would like for it to be.

Then take it one step farther and create a vision board. Get a large piece of poster board and cut out pictures and words of all that you want. If you can't find pictures or words of some items, type them up in large, colored letters. Then glue or tack all of these onto the poster board. This can be a work in progress. Add items or remove items as you see fit, but place this board where you will see it every day. Keep it in your bedroom and look at it when you go to bed every night. Think about having everything on the board in your life before falling asleep. By doing this, it will stimulate your senses and evoke positive feelings that will affect your body and mind in a positive manner and raise the frequencies of thought and send them into the universe.

Daily meditation will also help you to begin to see your future as you want it. This doesn't necessarily mean sitting cross-legged in a dark room with your palms up chanting *om* for an hour. There are simple ways to begin to meditate, and much of it is simply to practice moments of inward, private thinking.

One way is to just sit comfortably, or lie down comfortably somewhere. Set a goal to quiet your mind for five minutes. Relax your body. Start thinking about your toes and relaxing them, then your calves, your thighs, your hips, your back, belly, arms, fingers, neck and head. Relax every part of your body. Then try to clear your mind. Whenever a thought comes into your mind, let it dissipate like a cloud, or mentally create a chalkboard in your mind and erase the thought back to an empty black board. Once you quiet your mind for a few minutes, start visualizing and seeing your life as you want it. Maybe you think about having a new home or a new car. Maybe you focus on seeing your children happy doing things they love. Maybe you dream about a vacation you've always wanted to take. Whatever it may be, always see yourself in these thoughts as being happy, healthy and full of positive energy.

Always see yourself in your thoughts as being happy, healthy and full of positive energy.

There is another tool that can help you to meditate. It's a device that has earphones, eyeglasses and a digital recording that talks you through a meditative session. The earphones will allow you to listen to your instructor as well as to tune out outside noises. The eyeglasses will project a sequence of flashing lights that work with the neurotransmitters in your brain to help you relax. Then, a guiding voice will help you to meditate, relax, reduce stress, improve your wealth, balance your hormones and even help you with your tennis game if that's the program you choose. Regardless, this 20-minute session will put your body in a relaxed state so that when finished, your mind is very receptive to any positive input it may see or hear next. When the 20-minute session is completed, stay for ten more minutes and focus on what you want in your life.

Again, the more you can see your life as you want it, the sooner you will begin to attract it. Rhonda Byrne states in her book, *The Secret*, "You are the most powerful magnet in the universe. You contain magnetic power within you that is more powerful than anything in this world, and this unfathomable magnetic power is emitted through your thoughts."

When you emanate your dream on the inside of you in your thoughts, it will appear on the outside in your reality.

When you emanate your dream on the inside of you in your thoughts, it will appear on the outside in your reality. You have to *See* it to *Believe* it so you can *Achieve* it. You become what you think about! You achieve what you think about. Your *life* becomes what you think about. Think about making yours fulfilling, happy and peaceful.

Chapter 9: Seeing, Believing and Attracting

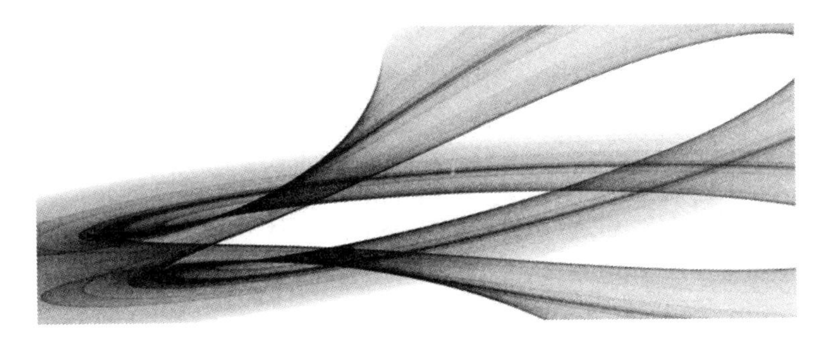

"See the things that you want as already yours. Know that they will come to you at need. Then let them come."
Robert Collier

While waiting for her six month appointment with Dr. Vida, Lumi's fingers quickly texted back and forth to Kara. Everything was great on both sides of the conversation.

"Mom," Kara texted, "You're always in such a good mood lately! What's going on? Have you met a man?" Then she followed her comment with a ☺ face.

Lumi laughed out loud. "No" she texted back, "but I'm not opposed to it! ☺"

"WOW! It's about time!" Kara responded. "Hey, guess what," Kara quickly moved on to her next thought. "Do you know your name means *light*? I was looking up names and that's what Lumi means."

"LOL" Lumi quickly text back. "Duh, yes!" she joked.

"I read that names reflect who you are. I guess it fits. You always seem to light up everyone else's lives because you're so positive all the time," Kara wrote.

"Thanks honey!" Lumi responded. Then she thought about how she was finally learning to let her inner light shine in order to be positive toward *herself,* not just others. She felt good inside! She also acknowledged what a caring and uplifting role model she had been for her children. She never really gave herself the credit she deserved, but with her changed outlook, she was beginning to accept proudly the good she had done for them and others. *It may have taken me over 40 years, but at least I'm finally learning,* she thought.

Actually Lumi was starting to feel much more positive about all areas of her life. Not only did she feel better mentally, but she looked wonderful! She was now at her perfect weight, had bought some new clothes that made her feel good, and felt better than she had in her twenties and thirties. She walked with more confidence, held her head up and always had a smile on her face. Writing made her feel good as well, and it seemed that she couldn't stop the connection between her thoughts and her fingers on the keypad of her computer lately. Words seemed to flow out of her like water out of a faucet, which excited her beyond measure.

Lumi looked up to see a middle-aged woman coming out of Dr. Vida's office. She quickly texted back to Kara, "Gotta go… am seeing Dr. Vida. Love you!" And she snapped her phone shut.

Dr. Vida approached Lumi and embraced her in a big hug. "How are you?" she asked.

"FABULOUS!" Lumi blurted out.

"Well, that's good to hear," Dr. Vida chuckled. "Let's take a look at the results of your blood test this week just to confirm that on paper."

Together they went over every item that was tested, and as Lumi felt, her blood work confirmed that she was, indeed, doing very well. They agreed that they would continue the same regimen for the next six months and then meet again to see if any adjustments would have to be made. "Just keep in mind," Dr. Vida reminded, "you know your body and mind better than anyone or any blood test could report. If you feel *funky*, you probably are, so come and see me earlier if you need to, but I think your days of feeling funky are over!"

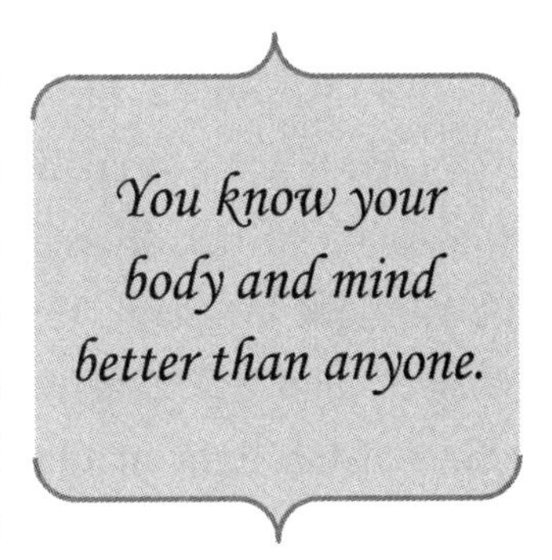

"I agree," Lumi responded as she got up to go. "I'll see you in six months." With that Lumi embraced Dr. Vida once again and whispered, "Thank you for everything."

Leaving Dr. Vida's office Lumi looked toward the lake at the end of the street. With the sun in her eyes, at first glance she thought she had just seen the luminescent image of an angel. She adjusted her sight and soon realized it was a light reflecting off a little girl's dress. As Lumi walked closer she could see the child was probably around five years old. She was dressed in a pink princess outfit, and on her head she wore a sparkling tiara! She was walking with her mother toward the park, twirling with every other step, which emphasized the sun's reflection even more. Lumi decided to follow in that direction and go to the park as well. She loved the lake and it was a good, tranquil place to sit and relax before she headed back home to her writing. Sitting there for a short time often inspired her with new ideas anyway.

She followed obligatory as though she were being led there by the little princess. As she got closer she could see the little girl's tiny pink ballet slippers skip up and down with each step and that glittery sequins covered every inch of her dress. They sparkled in all directions as the sunlight hit them. Her long blonde hair swayed as she twirled, also catching the rays of the sun, and her tiara reflected the light of the sun, which created a halo effect around her.

Lumi was captivated by this little girl, yet when almost to the park the little princess and her mother stopped and got into a nearby convertible. Lumi continued to walk forward and watched as the child crawled into the backseat. As her mother strapped her into her booster seat, she never took her eyes off of Lumi. She smiled the sweetest smile at Lumi. It was as if an angel just smiled at her. She then raised her arm high in the air and pointed her tiny finger toward the park with the same sweet smile. Lumi smiled back and gave a small wave as the car pulled out of its parking place. She watched the car drive away for a moment and then turned toward the lake where the child had pointed—toward her favorite park bench.

There was someone sitting there. It appeared to be a young man wearing jeans, a white T-shirt and a baseball cap. Lumi approached the bench anyway. There was plenty of room for two to sit; and besides, she was already there. This was her favorite spot to watch the ducks and sandhill cranes, and there were also two peacocks close by sunning themselves, which she always enjoyed watching. There was no way she was going to miss out on a few moments of this breathtaking and rejuvenating view.

As she got closer, however, she saw how intently this man was staring at the lake. She also noticed that he had one hand placed gently on an acoustic guitar that was leaning on the bench beside him. For a moment she almost turned away but then decided not to.

"Sorry to interrupt you, but do you mind if I sit here too?" Lumi asked politely.

The man gave a half-hearted smile and moved a bit to the right to make more room. He wasn't as young as Lumi first thought. He appeared to be closer to her age and was quite handsome. His black hair, with touches of a few stands of gray showed through where the baseball cap left off, and his dark green eyes had a sad and distant gloom to them.

Lumi sat quietly for a moment not wanting to interrupt whatever it was that he was thinking about. She, too, tried to engage in staring intently at the lake, but couldn't focus as the peacocks called out to one another with their shreaking squawks. But mostly she couldn't focus due to the sadness she felt coming from the other side of the bench. She glanced at him several times and then down at his guitar. In order to break the awkward silence she asked, "So, do you play?" knowing it was a stupid question but the first that popped into her head.

The man's head dropped, and his eyes moved from the lake to the ground. "Not well, apparently."

There was such discouragement and sadness in his voice. Lumi sensed that music must be very important to him and began, in typical Lumi fashion, to be encouraging, positive and optimistic. This was her innate nature, and it came out automatically when it came to helping others.

"Why?" Lumi asked with a soft and gentle concern. "Is there something wrong?"

Without answering he produced an envelope that Lumi hadn't noticed was there when she sat down. He reached inside and pulled out a CD of his songs and music. Then he pulled out a folded letter.

"My music was just rejected by this record company. I hoped...." He stopped speaking and there was a long pause. "Anyway, I guess I should have called myself the Pathetix!" Again, he took a long pause, "Maybe I'm pathetic for even thinking I had a chance."

"You know," Lumi responded, "you and your music are closer to being signed to a record label than so many others simply because you took the time to record it and risked rejection by these producers. Don't give up!"

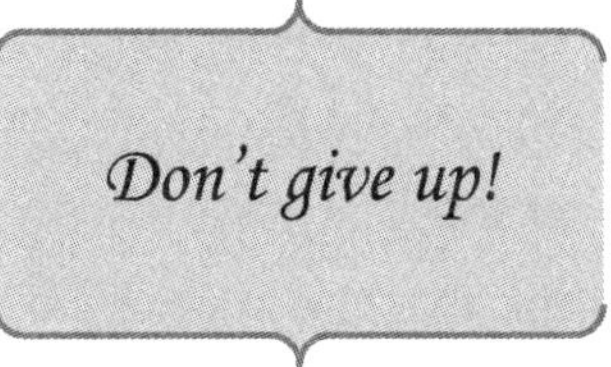

There were a few awkward moments of silence but Lumi felt compelled to ask, "Is music your passion? Do you feel this is what you're meant to do in life?"

"Yes," he replied as his green eyes looked directly at her.

If the dream is in your heart, it's meant to be there. You wouldn't have the dream if you didn't have the tools or ability to achieve it.

At that moment she realized how handsome he actually was, but she regained her focus and replied, "Then it's what you were meant to do. If the dream is in your heart, it's meant to be there. It isn't an accident or a mistake that it's there, and you wouldn't have the dream if you didn't have the tools or ability to achieve it."

He began to perk up a bit, so Lumi continued. "Have you ever heard the quote from Socrates, 'Be as you wish to seem'?"

"No," he replied seemingly interested.

"Well, do it! Be as you wish to seem. Be the person you see yourself being. If you see yourself as a successful musician and songwriter, then *be* that person. If that's the dream you have, and that's who you feel you are inside, then you've got to *see* yourself as that person and *do* what you think a person with those qualities would do. Do you think that the successful musicians you know ever quit? Of course not, or they wouldn't have become a success and we'd never have heard of them. There is no quitting when it comes to your dreams! There is only continuing to move forward no matter how many times you are knocked back or down. The only way for you to achieve your dream is to keep believing it and seeing it as already having happened. Then, and only then, will you see it manifesting in your outer reality."

The only way for you to achieve your dream is to keep believing it and seeing it as already having happened.

"You're right!" he said with more enthusiasm this time, and he extended his hand, "By the way, my name is Billy George."

"It's nice to meet you, Billy. I'm Lumi Powers," she responded as she placed her hand in his. As their hands met to shake, the warmth of his touch penetrated Lumi's heart. She felt such compassion for him. She had an understanding, beyond measure, of how he felt inside.

This, too, was how she felt about her writing. There were such self doubts and anxiety over whether or not she was good enough. She questioned if she was crazy to have the dream inside of her of writing a novel. She didn't know if she had enough talent or ability to achieve her dream; and she wasn't sure that, even if she did, she would have the courage to submit it to publishers or print it. At least Billy sent his music to a producer. He was farther along than she was, and here she was trying to give *him* advice! *Maybe I'm not here to give him advice, but to give myself some advice*, she thought.

"Do you think we actually have the ability to create the life we want?" he asked breaking her thoughts.

"Yes," Lumi responded immediately without thinking. "I do." She thought for a moment, "If we don't create our life, then who does? I think that we create our life by every choice we make. Today for example, you have the choice to give up and create one life, or try again and create another opportunity for the life you want."

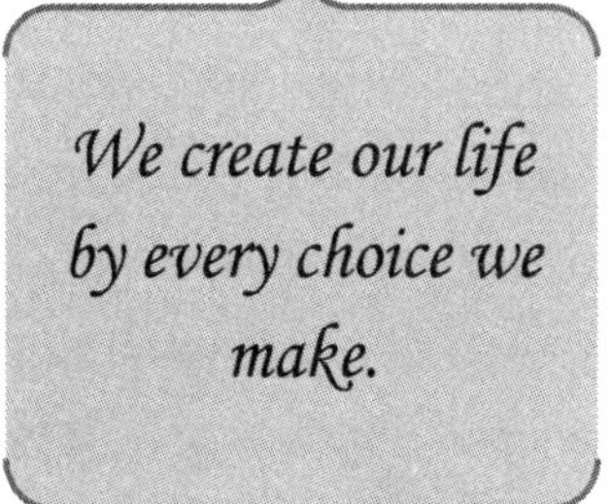

"I like that!" he said with even more enthusiasm.

"Socrates also said, 'The greatest way to live with honor in this world is to be what we pretend to be.' Actually the way I've always translated this was that you must live authentically. If you live your life based on who you are on the *inside,* and not just necessarily who you are on the outside, it's more honorable, and more fulfilling because it's who you're meant to be. You can't let others dictate who you are. If you did," Lumi paused, "then you'd be leaving the music you have on the inside of you on that piece of paper in your hand and in that envelope. Instead, I think it's time to let who you really are on the inside shine bright and let it come out through your music. You *are* who you *are* on the inside. Now it's time to express it on the *outside*!"

> *You are who you are on the inside. Express it on the outside!*

Then Lumi laughed. Billy was as wide-eyed as she was. "I honestly don't know where all these Socrates quotes are coming from!"

Billy laughed with her, "Well, wherever they're coming from, they're coming at the perfect time! You really have no idea...." He paused and more somberly remarked, "I was going to throw my guitar in the lake. I was so discouraged. I was ready to give up on my dream of who I believe I'm meant to be. You've helped me keep my dream alive and really brightened my day. Thank you so much." And again, he took Lumi's hand in his and held it gently.

The cry of a peacock interrupted the moment, and Lumi pulled her hand from his as she stood up from the bench. "It's been a pleasure, Billy George. I'm sure it won't be long before I hear your music on the radio and think, *I met him one day on 7th Avenue."*

Billy rose to say goodbye as well, and as Lumi walked away, she heard him call to her, "Thank you again. I'm so happy I met you."

That night Lumi lay in bed thinking about Billy and his music. *I have to take my own advice. If I'm going to be an author, then I need to do what an author would do and get my book published. Tomorrow I'm going to start looking into publishers and submit a proposal.*

Illumination

The lotus flower begins to grow submerged in the mud in the bottom of a pond. As it slowly rises to bloom, it is untouched and unscathed by the impurities of the mud and muck it begins in. Once it reaches the surface, it blossoms and turns into an exquisite, beautiful flower. It is then that it miraculously has the ability to transform the dirty water in which it exists. The water becomes much clearer and more transparent around it, which allows for more light to flow into the pond, which ultimately allows for more life-giving energy to enter the pond.

It doesn't matter that the lotus flower appears to be a mud flower initially. It knows innately who it is inside and rises little-by-little, overcoming all obstacles that it meets on its way. It doesn't allow the mud or muck to cling to it, though it might be easy for it to fall into the trap of thinking that if that's the environment it's in, then that's where it's meant to be. But instead, it knows its destiny. It knows who it is on the inside and continues on its path to become that. It isn't always easy, but the belief of knowing its purpose in life *inside* helps it to press on to become that on the *outside*. Once finally reaching the surface, it expresses both on the inside *and* outside all that it is meant to be; and as a result, everything around it benefits. Lao Tzu describes it as letting go of where you are in order to become what you might be.

Everyone is born with a purpose—a dream that is placed in his or her heart. Many people forget their dreams early on. Many pursue them until they run into obstacles and it becomes too difficult. But many don't forget, and it is those who achieve great life satisfaction because they let their inner dream manifest into reality on the outside.

Everyone is born with a purpose—a dream that is placed in his or her heart.

You, too, were born with a purpose and dream. Do you remember what it is? Do you have regrets that you put it on the back burner at one point in your life? Did you give up on your dream somewhere along the line? Maybe you don't really know what your purpose is. Maybe you don't have a burning passion of a dream in your belly.

Many women in their forties are faced with reflecting back on their lives in order to try to figure out what their purpose actually is. It can be discouraging thinking that you may not have a grand purpose in life or anything that you are passionate about. If that's the case, you simply have a bit of clouded vision, because you *do* have a purpose!

The famous philosopher, Lao Tzu, stated, "At the center of your being you have the answer; you know who you are and what you want." So get a pen and three pieces of paper. On the first page begin to write down lists and lists of all the wonderful traits and abilities you have. List your talents and your interests.

> *"At the center of your being you have the answer; you know who you are and what you want."*
> *Lao Tzu*

On the second piece of paper make a list of all the things you wanted to do, or still want to do, in your life.

On the third piece of paper describe yourself, not as you are, but as the person you want to be. Describe the perfect you! Describe exactly how you want to look. *(Okay, but let's be real here. No describing that you want to look like another person but instead, describe the best you that you want to be.)* Describe your perfect personality when you are absolutely at your best and the happiest. Write about things that you enjoy doing and how you would do them. Describe the type of people you would associate with and how you would interact with them and how they would make you feel. Remember, only positive relationships should be described. Describe how you would live your life. Describe your home, your family, your surroundings, your work, and everything that comes to mind.

You are creating an architectural plan for your life and for who you will be. See it as you want it to be. When you are done, read it over and see if there is any one area that really excites you. It's okay if there isn't, because as you start to move toward creating this picture, your life purpose will begin to become clearer. When you live authentically in an environment that creates harmony with who you are on the inside and how you are living on the outside, it will begin to not only benefit you and move you toward realizing who you really are, but it will also benefit others.

You are creating an architectural plan for your life and for who you will be.

When you start to live based on who you were created to be, you will find that it affects others around you in a positive manner. Just like the lotus flower's ultimate existence allows for more light to flow into the pond which creates life-giving energy to enter, you, too, will begin to allow your inner light to shine for others. You will automatically emit an inner positive light of energy for others.

Everyone has felt, at one time or another, someone's negative energy. When you live a life of purpose you only emit positive, life-giving energy to all those around you. I guarantee someone will say to you, "What are you doing? There is a change about you."

People will feel it. But more than that, the universe will feel it.

The universe is a huge energy field, and within this energy field, like attracts like. You will attract what you put out. Whatever you see, believe and *feel*, you will attract to you. If you put out energy feelings of discouragement, unhappiness and frustration, then you will attract more situations into your life that will give you *more* of these feelings. The energy you emit attracts energy from the universe to match it. Though you may think that this is a bit *out there*, just keep in mind that at one time everyone believed the world to be flat! Most people live in a very restricted circle of belief and potentiality. Keep your mind open to the belief that just because you can't see it, doesn't mean that it doesn't exist.

Whatever you see, believe and feel, you will attract to you.

Change your attitude from negative to positive. Release the constraints of your limited thinking. Let go of past hurts and self-depreciating thoughts. Feed your mind with positives. Express your talents. Emit the feelings of happiness, gratitude, fulfillment, and see opportunity and abundance in all areas of your life. As a result, that is what you will attract from the universe. The universe will respond to you by providing situations that give you more of what you express. The universe is a constantly moving current of energy. Everything circulates and creates circular motion. If you give good, it will circle back to you. If you give off negativity, it will circle back to you.

No person is given a life purpose that is bad for him or her. God is all good, so when you live authentically and on purpose, you automatically produce nothing but positive, good things in your life. So dream the life you desire. You have the power and ability within you to create your own reality. Change what isn't working and manifest the life you want. As Corin Nemec stated, "Never let life impede on your ability to manifest your dreams. Dig deeper into your dreams and deeper into yourself and believe that anything is possible, and make it happen."

Dream the life you desire. You have the ability within you to create your own reality.

Chapter Ten: Six Months Later…

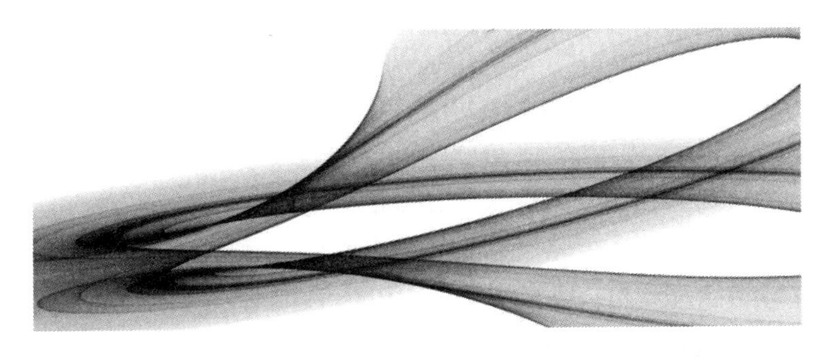

"Everyone has a spirit that can be refined, a body that can be trained in some manner, a suitable path to follow. You are here to realize your inner divinity and manifest your innate enlightenment."
Morihei Ueshiba

Lumi's phone began vibrating quickly on the table as it played, *Oh Happy Day*! She glanced at the screen to see Kara's name. She picked it up quickly.

"Happy Birthday, Mom!" she heard both Kyle and Kara yell on the speakerphone. Then together they sang, "Happy Birthday to you, Happy Birthday to you, Happy Birthday dear Mo-o-m, Happy Birthday to you!"

Lumi laughed, "Thanks!"

Kara yelled as if Lumi couldn't hear her well on the speaker, "We'll be home this weekend, and then we can take you out for dinner to celebrate if that's okay."

"Sounds perfect!" Lumi responded.

"So what are you doing to celebrate today, Mom?" Kyle asked.

"I think I'm going to 7th Avenue, do a little shopping and maybe grab lunch. Tonight I was planning on playing a little tennis with the girls."

"Well, have fun, and we'll see you on Friday night. Gotta go to class. Talk to you soon. Love you, and HAPPY BIRTHDAY!" they chimed in together.

"Love you too," Lumi said as they all hung up the phones.

She glanced at the calendar on the wall. Where had the year gone? It felt as though it was only yesterday that she had her last birthday. So much had happened since then. She realized that Dr. Vida was instrumental in her life over the past year and was largely responsible for how good she was feeling. She had learned so much about her body, hormones and nutrients. She thought of all the other lessons she learned over the past year as well. So much of it had changed her perception of herself and her thinking. She worked hard to focus her mind on the positive instead of the negative, which now felt second nature to her. She also worked to get back into shape physically, which included playing tennis once again. She was enjoying the company of her friends more often, which was very fulfilling. There was so much she was thankful for. She also finally redecorated her bedroom and remodeled her bath to include the Jacuzzi for two that she wanted. But most important of all, she finally finished her novel. Today, to celebrate her birthday, she was going to 7th Avenue to drop the final draft into the mail to the *very* interested publishing company who had agreed to print and publish it! She was now a real published author!

Lumi was both excited and nervous. She picked up the large FedEx package from the table and re-checked the address, flipped it over and made sure the seal was secure once again. She then headed to the door with the package and her purse in hand. She paused at the foyer mirror before opening the front door and peered into it.

There will be no more funk for you. It's all going to be fabulous from here on!

"Happy Birthday, Lumi. There will be no more *funk* for you. It's all going to be fabulous from here on!" She giggled to herself and thought, *Well, maybe a little funk—so how about FUNKABULOUS!* She then spoke out loud once again, "This is going to be your best year yet!" She glanced at the plaque hanging below the mirror that said, *Good Things are Going to Happen! That's right*, she thought with confidence.

She smiled at herself knowing how true her statement was—well at least she knew it had the *potential* to be her best year yet! If she really believed in that statement, and her actions and feelings corresponded to that thought, it definitely could be! And Lumi was determined to see that it would be. She pulled her sunglasses from her bag and put them on, gave another quick glance in the mirror and headed to 7th Avenue.

Lumi was almost shaking as she parallel-parked in front of the FedEx store on 7th Avenue. She checked to make sure she wasn't too far from the curb, shut the car off and then picked up her envelope once again. She sat quietly for a moment clutching the package in her lap staring forward. She took a deep breath and thought, *it's time, Lumi Powers*, and left the car.

She walked to the FedEx door and pushed it open and proceeded to the counter.

"Good morning, Ma'am," the scruffy man behind the counter said as he greeted her with a big smile.

"Good morning," Lumi smiled back.

"You have a package for us I see."

"Yes," Lumi responded as she laid it gently in front of him.

"Let me weigh this and get it out for you."

Lumi watched him intently as he weighed the package and then starting tapping information into his computer.

"That will be $16.58 and will arrive in New York tomorrow by noon. Is that okay?" he asked.

"That will be perfect," Lumi responded, "Absolutely perfect."

She felt a rush of adrenaline flow through her body and an inexplicable sense of happiness. The book she always wanted to write was now written. It took a constant belief in herself and her abilities, as well as the belief that it would actually be published. By focusing on these beliefs day-in and day-out, she began to see the book as written and published. This helped her to take the steps necessary to achieve and accomplish it, such as writing daily. All of which led to the manifestation of her greatest desire—writing a novel and having it published. She had envisioned this moment for months.

She paid for the shipping and left the store with lightness in her step and her inner light shining brightly through the smile she carried. She couldn't remember the last time she had felt this good.

It was a beautiful day, and Lumi decided to do a little window-shopping. She took her time as she soaked up the warmth of the sun as she walked down the street and thought about her upcoming trip to New York just two weeks away. This was when she would be reviewing the layout and cover design of her book. Kyle and Kara were joining her on the trip as well. They had planned on making it a mini-vacation, and she couldn't wait to show them the sites of New York and take them for a carriage ride through Central Park. Her thoughts, however, were interrupted and she stopped abruptly in front of *Ray's Music Store*. There in the window was a poster that caught her eye. *That's Billy George*, she thought. There, on a huge poster in the window, was a picture of Billy and his new album, *The Secret on 7th Avenue*. Lumi's heart skipped a beat. *Was this really the Billy she met in the park that day?* The poster didn't lie. There he was holding up his new CD with its #1 hit – *Ancient Ways*.

Lumi couldn't wait to go inside and almost knocked someone over as she burst through the door. She scanned the room quickly looking for headphones. She knew you could always listen to songs and albums at *Ray's*. And there they were, headphones, lined up next to the counter, hanging above four neatly arranged bar stools. Heading directly to them she turned to a young boy who obviously worked there and asked, "Can I listen to *Ancient Ways* for a minute?"

"Of course," he responded. "It's already programmed in the first seat. Just hit play."

Lumi sat on the scratched up wooden barstool, placed the headphones on her ears and hit play. The music stirred her soul. Then she heard a voice that was faintly familiar to her as Billy sang the words of a meeting he had with a woman who quoted Socrates. A tear ran down Lumi's face. *He didn't give up on becoming who he was born to be.*

She thought back to their meeting almost a year ago in the park, and a smile came to her face. She was so happy for him. She removed the headphones and hung them back on the hook in front of her. She scanned the store to see where his CD might be. Prominently displayed at the front of the store was a large poster and stack of CDs. She picked one up and looked it over. Then she picked up two more. *Kyle and Kara will love this, too,* she thought.

So excited she was almost giddy, she paid the cashier for her three CDs.

"Why don't you get those signed before you go," the cashier remarked.

"What do you mean?" Lumi asked.

"I'd be happy to sign them for you," she heard from a voice over her shoulder. It was the same sweet voice that she heard on the CD.

Lumi turned abruptly to see Billy George standing a few inches from her. Smiling ear to ear like he had just won a prize at a fair, he exclaimed, "Lumi Powers! It's you!"

"You remember me?" Lumi asked in amazement.

"This album was inspired by you. I've thought of you every day since we met! I went to the park so many times to see if you would show up, but you never did. So I focused on my music and all that you said to me, and this…" holding up a CD, "is a result of that."

"I don't know what to say," Lumi responded dumbfoundedly.

With a boyish charm he replied, "How about saying you would love to have lunch with me today while I sign your CDs."

Lumi smiled and responded, "I'd love to."

Billy reached out to take her hand in his. Their eyes locked and Lumi knew she was right. *This was going to be a great year!*

"If you believe in something, and believe in it long enough, it will come into being."
Rolling Thunder

Illumination

Looking at a caterpillar you may only see a small, fuzzy, slug-like character crawling around in a limited area of existence. You can't see its potential or the opportunity it has to transform, spread its wings and fly. You may think that it's incapable of becoming a butterfly by looking at it in its current state. And you'd be right *if* the caterpillar believed it would always be a caterpillar. If that were the case, it never would wrap itself in a cocoon and enter a larval stage. But it knows innately who it is on the inside, sees it and believes it can happen, and then takes steps in order to reach its full potential, transform and fly.

Every step you take to live your life's purpose, become a better human being, and a more positive person, transforms you as well. This transformation can be as great as the transformation a caterpillar makes. The potential is unlimited. You have the ability to transform your life into one that is fabulous—which is mostly done by changes to your thoughts, beliefs and attitudes.

You have the ability to transform your life into one that is fabulous—which is mostly done by changes to your thoughts, beliefs and attitudes.

Possibilities are endless. There are no limits to your transformation, and you'll be amazed at how quickly it can take place. The inner joy you will feel as you take each step forward is indescribable. The positive changes and events that will take place in your life will amaze you. Once you experience a mere taste of how this mentality will change your life, you will never go back to your old ways of thinking.

Michelangelo stated, "The greater danger for most of us lies not in setting our aim too high and falling short, but in setting our aim too low and achieving our mark." Don't set your expectations and dreams too low. Dream big dreams! Dream of happiness. Don't sell yourself short. Women tend to do this as they get older. Yet, when they were a five-year-old they had no limitations to their dreams. They were happy and believed all was possible. Find those feelings inside of you again. Your natural birthright is for you to be happy and to achieve the dreams inside of you. There should be no limits to your dreams. Ronald Reagan stated, "There are no constraints on the human mind, no walls around the human spirit, no barriers to our progress except those we ourselves erect." Don't create self-imposed barriers and constraints. Go for it. Believe that anything is possible.

But more than anything, now is the time to *be happy*. All *Illuminations* in this book lead to one common lesson: focusing on being happy *now*! Utilize the *Illuminations* in order to achieve this happiness. Don't wait until tomorrow to be happy. Don't wait for: *I'll be happy when…* Don't wait for: *I'll be happy if…* There is *no* waiting for happiness.

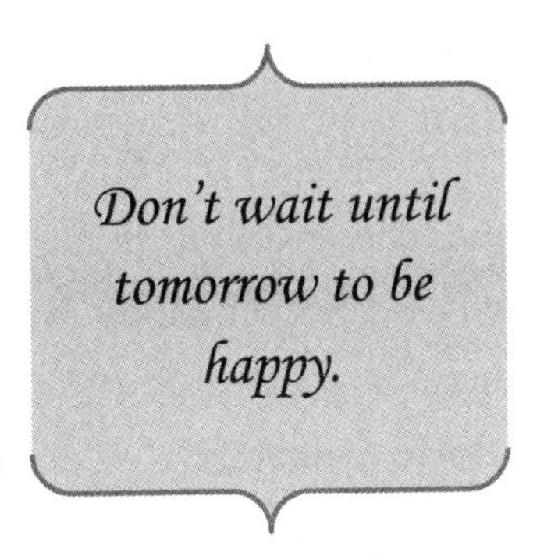

Happiness is a choice and a state of being. It doesn't come from outside or external things, actions or people. It comes from within. It starts in your thoughts and is expressed by your feelings. This is why your thoughts are so important. You can choose to focus on the good in your life, the things you are grateful for, the kindness you practice and the good qualities of all the relationships you are in. All of which will assist you with happy thoughts and good feelings.

Then by practicing visualization you will see the good and happiness you want in your life and will believe that it will transpire. Again, this helps you to focus on things that make you feel good inside.

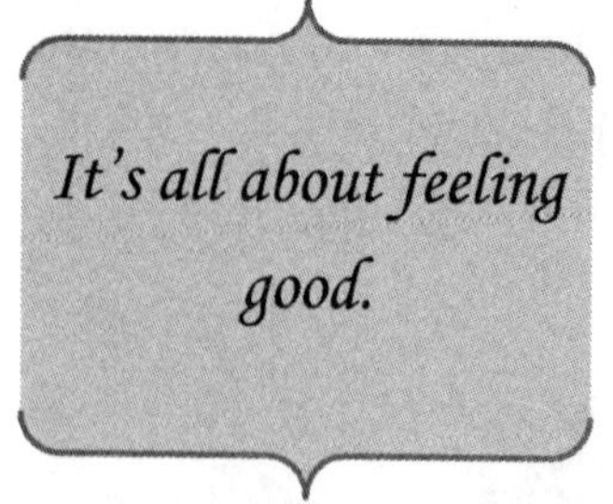

It's all about feeling good! If there's one thing that you do, and nothing else, it's to monitor how you are feeling on a regular basis throughout the day. *Are you feeling happy?* If not, change your thoughts and focus on something that *makes* you feel happy. See the good in everything, because there *is* good in everything. You simply have to make a choice to see it.

Aristotle states, "Happiness depends upon ourselves." You can make excuses as to why you aren't happy and then be unhappy; or you can choose to be happy regardless of all external circumstances. Choosing happiness is the most powerful way to transform your life.

Choosing happiness is the most powerful way to transform your life.

The universe has unlimited ways to bring to you more and more of what you feel. When you focus on feeling happy on a continuous basis, you will get more of it in your life. Your cup will overflow! Then the universe will fill that cup with more whether you carry a little, medium or gigantic cup! Choose to carry the largest cup you can.

If you *feel* happy, you *will* transform your life, and everything around you will transform in order to provide you more of it.

This is *your* time to transform, achieve your dreams, live the life you imagined and be happier than you ever believed possible. It's time to let go of the *funk* and start living your life in a *fabulous* manner. You *are* who you choose to *be*. Choose to be *Funkabulous!*

ILLUMINATING QUOTES

Illuminating Quotes

A man is but the product of his thoughts. What he thinks, he becomes.

Mohandas Gandhi

The state of your life is nothing more than a reflection of your state of mind.

Dr. Wayne W. Dyer

We are what we think. All that we are arises with our thoughts.

Buddha

Change your thoughts, and you change your world.

Norman Vincent Peale

You create your own universe as you go along.

Winston Churchill

Therefore I tell you, whatever you ask for in prayer, believe that you have received it, and it will be yours.

Jesus Christ, the Bible, Mark 11:24

Imagination is everything. It is the preview of life's coming attractions.

Albert Einstein

You have the power and ability to create your own reality – to change what isn't working and to manifest what you desire.

Dick Sutphen

I found that when you start thinking and saying what you really want, your mind automatically shifts and pulls you in that direction. And sometimes it can be that simple, just a little twist in vocabulary that illustrates your attitude and philosophy.

Jim Rohn

We cannot become what we want to be by remaining what we are.

Max DePree

The only limit to our realization of tomorrow will be our doubts of today.

Franklin D. Roosevelt

Whatever the mind can conceive it can achieve.

W. Clement Stone

The first principle of achievement is mental attitude. Man begins to achieve when he begins to believe.

J.C. Roberts

You become what you think about.

Earl Nightingale

Everybody is a magnet. You attract to yourself reflections of that which you are. If you're friendly, then everybody else seems to be friendly too.

Dr. David Hawkins

By your thoughts you are daily, even hourly, building your life; you are carving your destiny.

Ruth Barrick Golden

Think and feel yourself there! To achieve any aim in life, you need to project the end-result. Think of the elation, the satisfaction, the joy! Carrying the ecstatic feeling will bring the desired goal into view.

Grace Speare

As you think, so shall you become.

Bruce Lee

You are where your thoughts have brought you; you will be tomorrow where your thoughts take you.

James Allen

Never let life impede on your ability to manifest your dreams. Dig deeper into your dreams and deeper into yourself and believe that anything is possible and make it happen.

Corin Nemic

The greatest discovery in a hundred years was the discovery that man has within himself the power to control his surroundings, that he is not at the mercy of chance or luck, that he is the arbiter of his own fortunes, and that he can carve out his own destiny.

William James

The best way to predict the future is to create it.

Peter Drucker

Everything lives, moves, everything corresponds; the magnetic rays, emanating either from myself or from others, cross the limitless chain of created things.

Gerard De Nerval

Hold a picture of yourself long and steadily enough in your mind's eye, and you will be drawn toward it.

Napoleon Hill

You are embarking on the greatest adventure of your life—to improve your self-image, to create more meaning in your life and in the lives of others. This is your responsibility. Accept it, now!

Maxwell Maltz

Bibliography

Aesop. "The Lion and the Mouse." 27 Aug. 2010. http://www.aesopfables.com/cgi/aesopl.cgi?e&TheLion&theMouse.jpg.

Byrne, Rhonda. The Secret. New York: Atria Books: Beyond Words, 2006.

Chopra, Deepak. 27 Aug. 2010. "Deepak Chopra Quotes." http://thinkexist.com/Quotes/deepak_chopra/.

"Faith," Webster Dictionary.

Pati, Sangeeta, MD, FACOG. "Should We Be Without Hormones." 27 Aug. 2010. http://sajune.com/medical_center_bioidentical_hormone.html.

Payne, Peggy, and Allan Luks. The Healing Power of Doing Good. Iuniverse, 2001.

About the Author

Ivy Gilbert is an entrepreneur, the owner of several companies, a Certified Life Coach, and has written or edited over twenty books.

Her coaching and consulting practices use a combination of goal-setting, philosophy and personally developed processes that are inspired by the Law of Attraction to help empower and inspire her clients to create abundance and success in every area of their lives. She has always had a relentless commitment to personal growth and achievement and utilizes the knowledge she has accumulated to assist her clients with their personal goals and endeavors.

Ivy's background has included 25 years in business with an extensive concentration in finance, management, sales and business development. She had one of the largest financial planning practices in the country and received numerous accolades (including the Woman of Distinction Award) from many organizations for her dedication to women's financial independence. For the past twelve years she has worked as a consultant, and over the last year her efforts have been focused on building a solar energy company. Ivy has also been a featured speaker at seminars around the country and was a regular guest speaker on cable TV.

She has a business degree from Thomas College, a degree in counseling from United Church Ministries International, and a degree from Franklin Pierce University.

To contact the author you can email her at:
ivy@funkabulous.com

To receive newsletters and periodic emails sign up at:
www.funkabulous.com

Barry Myers
7th Avenue CD

7th Avenue is original music by singer/songwriter, Barry Myers. The album is adult, contemporary rock inspired by the themes of the book, *Feeling Funkabulous.*

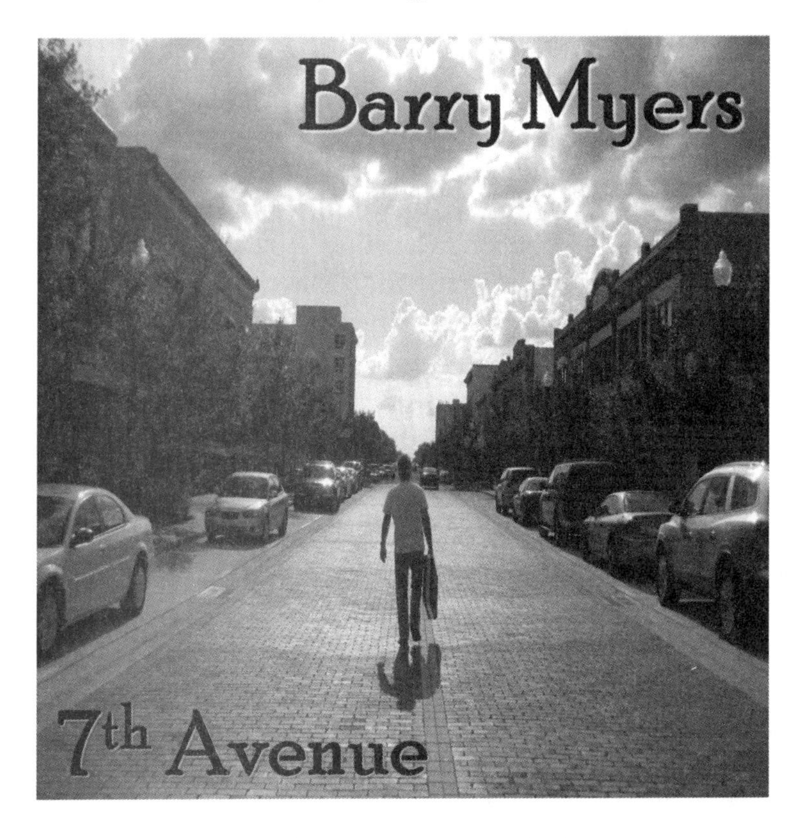

Order the CD today by going to www.funkabulous.com or download the CD to your iPod or MP3 player at all participating retail outlets: iTunes, Amazon and CD Baby.

Creative Visualization and Relaxation Trainer - NXTLynk

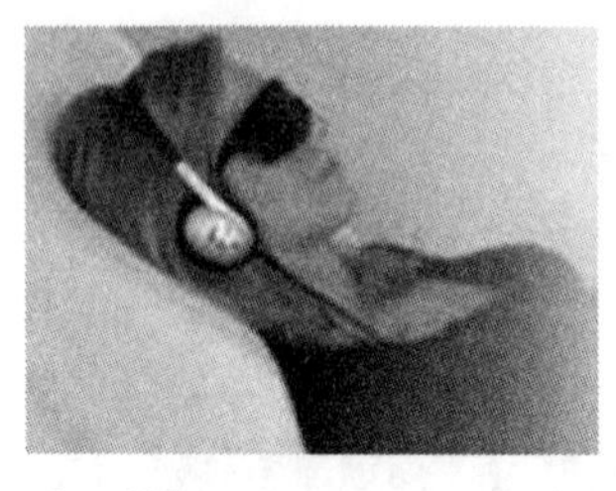

The light and sound technology in the NXTLynk guides your mind into a desired meditative state—the perfect state for making life changes such as losing weight, vanquishing a bad habit, creating the life you want, and more. This is done through pulses of light and sound set at the frequency of the desired state of mind. The NXTLynk is a powerful combination of MP3 player, light and sound relaxation system, and personal program guide and is designed to make meditation nearly effortless.

Mind Over Menopause

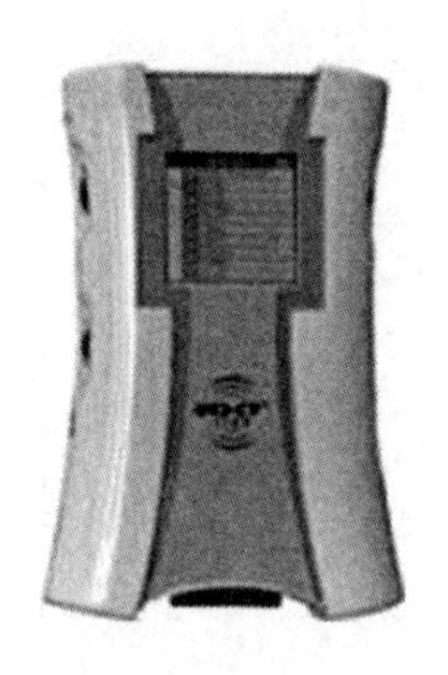

Balancing Your Life
Obtaining Harmony During this Life Cycle
Mastering Menopause
Controlling Night Sweats and Hot Flashes
Eliminating Brain Fog and Improving Your Memory
Balancing Emotional and Physical Changes During Menopause
Staying Centered In Times of Uncertainty
Increasing Your Energy and Releasing Fatigue
Mastering Menopause and the Physical Changes that Occur
Tips for Quick Menopause Relief
And more...

For more information or to order your own Creative Visualization and Relaxation Trainer, go to www.funkabulous.com